SEEKERSTAR

STAR TRIBES: BOOK TWO

BLAZE WARD

KNOTTED ROAD PRESS

SeekerStar
Star Tribes, Book Two
Blaze Ward
Copyright © 2020 Blaze Ward
All rights reserved
Published by Knotted Road Press
www.KnottedRoadPress.com

ISBN: 978-1-64470-139-3

Cover art:

ID 78375918 © Philcold | Dreamstime.com

Cover and interior design copyright © 2020 Knotted Road Press

Never miss a release!
If you'd like to be notified of new releases, sign up for my newsletter.

I will never spam you, or use your email for nefarious purposes. You can also unsubscribe at any time.

http://www.blazeward.com/newsletter/

Star Tribes

WinterStar

SeekerStar

SeptStar

SwiftStar

MorningStar

The Handsome Rob Gigs

Can't Shoot Straight Gang

Can't Shoot Straight Gang Returns

Hunting Handsome Rob

The Jessica Keller Chronicles

Auberon

Queen of the Pirates

Last of the Immortals

Goddess of War

Flight of the Blackbird

The Red Admiral

St. Legier

Winterhome

Petron

CS-405

Queen Anne's Revenge

Packmule

Persephone

Additional Alexandria Station Stories

Siren

Two Bottles of Wine with a War God

The Story Road

The Science Officer Series

The Science Officer

The Mind Field

The Gilded Cage

The Pleasure Dome

The Doomsday Vault

The Last Flagship

The Hammerfield Gambit

The Hammerfield Payoff

Shadow of the Dominion

Longshot Hypothesis

Hard Bargain

Outermost

Dominion-427

Phoenix

Princess Rualoh

Earth Force Sky Patrol

Birth of the Star Dragon

Flight of the Star Dragon

Call of the Star Dragon

Shadow of the Star Dragon

Trial of the Star Dragon

PART ONE
SCHOLAR

ONE

Daniel studied the two books before him, one written in the common Spacer that humans had taken with them into the galaxy, the other in a script he had never seen before he encountered the book in a junk store six months before.

Nobody else on the ship could read it. And probably nobody within several thousand light-years. The script was as alien as anything he had ever heard of, let alone seen.

Not Latin characters. Nor *Rabic*. Vaguely similar to Chinese ideograms, but written left to right instead of vertically. And denser in their construction, most characters having six brush strokes at a minimum, plus the one on the first page containing twenty-two.

Now that the K'bari ghost in his mind had shown him how to read the book, Daniel knew those twenty-two strokes represented the name of the author who had compiled a history of K'bari galactic exploration. And that he had done so about the same time that humans were building their first industrial facilities for the mass production of metals on Earth, in places like the tiny peninsula of Europe back on the homeworld.

The K'bari homeworld didn't exist, anymore. The being that Daniel occasionally impersonated had destroyed it during his ten thousand years of terror and conquest across the galaxy.

Urid-Varg. The Conqueror. *Violeur.*

Destroyer of dreams and peoples.

Rapist.

Daniel reached out a hand for the mug of coffee that had gone cold as he had finished off the last of the translation.

Urid-Varg had encountered the K'bari at some point in the distant past. After he wiped out the entire z'lud over the course of a thousand years. Not that far in the past, either.

Daniel sipped the last of the cold coffee and looked around the communal dining hall aboard *WinterStar* where he normally served meals to Kathra Omezi's comitatus. Three tables with benches facing each other, space for forty friendly women. A long table where bins would go for each woman to walk along and select the food that would fuel her and provide her joy for the day.

After more than a year aboard the vessel *WinterStar*, Daniel Lémieux was still the only male that called this ship home. Others came and went as they were needed for various tasks, but they lived aboard one of the other ships that made up the Commander's tribal squadron.

The Mbaysey Tribe. Twenty-two ClanStars. Two *WaterStars. ForgeStar. IronStar.*

And *WinterStar*, like a sheepdog protecting all of them from coyotes, pirates, and scouts from the Sept Empire looking to return these women to the fold.

The Commander had ordered Daniel to complete the translation as a priority, assigning Ndidi as his permanent *Sous Chef* here in the kitchen, to feed the women while he worked. Perhaps the youngster was now *Chef de Cuisine* and Daniel had been quietly promoted to Executive Chef when he wasn't looking. Still in charge, technically, but just a pretty face around the kitchen, rather than the one making decisions.

After all, they were all in safe hands with Ndidi cooking.

She wasn't his rival for skill yet, but he could see her getting there in another year or two. Certainly, at nineteen she was already his peer in the kitchen. He would eventually need to take her someplace rough though, like Nice, or maybe even Brest on the Homeworld itself, and open a bistro with her, in order to toughen the woman up, bring her fully to the level of business acumen that would make her his equal in all things.

Someplace where you literally had to walk down to the docks each evening and charm the fishermen for their catch before someone else could buy it. Or cultivate the insular, sour farmers who might let you know when the really good vegetables were due, so you could fix them a little something special as a bribe.

With the Mbaysey, the various clans really couldn't withhold the good things when they sent the regular tithe and trade goods to the other ships and *WinterStar*. The *WaterStars* sent fish as they were supposed to, but Commander Omezi kept them on a short leash anyway.

Ndidi would need to spend time with folks who could tell her no if they wanted to, and laugh in her face about it.

The hatch to the main corridor opened as Daniel decided he needed more coffee and stood up. A lone figure filled the doorway, looking around until she found him.

Kathra Omezi. Commander of the Mbaysey Tribal Squadron. At just twenty-nine years old, she was already a wily veteran who had stepped into her mother's space seven years ago and protected the rest of the women here from the Sept Empire. And they were mostly women.

Modern medicine meant that the Commander could

maintain an overall population that was eighty-five percent female. Eighty percent of births, with an expectation that some males would leave forever when they were old enough to return to places where men were generally in charge.

Those that remained found softer jobs to fill. Teachers. Assistants. Artists.

Kathra's warriors and mechanics were all female. Her entire comitatus was, as well.

Save for one of the two chefs.

Daniel stepped away from the table with an empty coffee mug in hand and went to the samovar.

"Your timing is, of course, perfect," he smiled up at her as she entered.

Daniel had to look up in order to see her face. At one hundred and seventy centimeters, he was short for a male. At one hundred and ninety-five, Kathra was taller than most of the men he had known. Most of the comitatus looked down on Daniel as well.

At least physically. That is, they were all taller.

Maybe not tougher, but Daniel had grown up in kitchens, where the squeamish and cowardly didn't last long. Had eventually started his own bistro, back on Genarde. Sold it and started a second later.

Earned the coveted Golden Diamond from Gastropode magazine with *Pain du Soir*, his second bistro. Been famous and wealthy and in demand.

And had a nervous breakdown.

Or maybe an angry breakdown.

Sold that place to his *Sous Chef* for the thousand Sept Crowns the man had in his wallet at that moment, walked out the front door, and never once bothered to look back.

It had landed him here. With her.

Kathra smiled at him as she approached.

"Perfect, you say?" she smiled, white teeth appearing against onyx-black skin like stars coming out at night.

The woman moved like a great cat stalking, but Daniel was not her prey this morning.

He hoped.

"It is done," Daniel said simply, gesturing to the two books on the table.

He turned his attention to the samovar and withdrew enough coffee to keep him going.

As men got older, they were supposed to put on weight as their metabolism slowed. He supposed that channeling the mental powers of Urid-Varg was the reason he had lost even the trace of a spare tire he had once had around his middle.

That and healthy eating. And plenty of exercise. He was in better shape now than he had ever been in his life, but on a good day there still wasn't a woman in the comitatus that couldn't wrap him around a chair without working up a sweat.

Unless he cheated.

Daniel turned when Kathra didn't answer. She had sat down across the table from where he had been before and turned the notebook around to where she could read it.

Daniel slowly returned to his warm chair and sat, sucking down heat and liquid as the woman focused on her reading.

It made him feel ancient to realize that at thirty-eight, he was one of the oldest people on the ship, and far and away the oldest person in the comitatus, in spite of all the other women adopting him.

He sipped for a time and considered mortality. His, and everyone else's.

"Can we find them?" she looked up and interrupted his musing.

Daniel shrugged as eloquently as he could.

"Does a star-born species ever actually die out?" he asked.

"I can see their culture dying, if you get to be too small as a group and disappear into a larger one. And perhaps eventually they end up living in barrios or ghettos until they rebound, or simply fade away."

"You have given this a great deal of thought," she observed with a grin.

"Our ancestors were just understanding the industrial revolution when this K'bari scholar sat down to look back at several thousand years of their history in space and highlight some of the interesting things they had done and seen."

"Does he have a name?" Kathra asked. "Do either of them?"

Either of them? Ah, she meant the ghost who lived inside his head. The one who had stepped out of the background when Daniel opened this book and showed him how to read it.

There were a thousand ghosts in his head, left there when he had mastered the gem that Urid-Varg had used to amplify his powers. That *salaud* would take over the mind of a new victim with his powers before he embedded the gem—housing his own soul and mind—into their body, riding it for a time until that flesh got too old and Urid-Varg moved on to the next.

And the next.

Twelve thousand years as a vampire. Or whatever it was he was.

Daniel lacked the vocabulary to describe the creature accurately.

No, that wasn't true.

Violeur. That covered the *salaud* just fine.

Daniel turned his mind inward to see the K'bari ghost standing in the foreground, where he had been for the weeks it took to translate this book, with all the others choosing perhaps to step back a little and let the man work.

Three eyes across the face, with the nose below that stretched outward into a furry snout halfway between feline and canine for size.

Green eyes. Yellowish-tan fur.

The being had petite horns that swept back from his forehead and outward, rather like an ox, rather than backwards like a deer or a demon.

And a wan, sad smile.

"We do not have the right vocal cords," Daniel explained as he looked back to Kathra. "I call him Arsène. It is close enough to the name he had before Urid-Varg. The scholar I call *Idir*, which means *Alive* in the ancient Berber tongue and is a close enough transliteration of his name."

"I see," she nodded, closing the book back up and sliding it towards him. "Should we seek them?"

Daniel didn't bother hiding his surprise. He had fancied exotic quests for the K'bari, but never actually imagined Kathra would seriously consider doing such a thing.

He had never been good at lying to women, and Kathra Omezi already seemed to have a sixth sense for that sort of thing anyway, so he just shrugged.

"I know what stars they claimed two thousand years ago," Daniel offered softly. "But we are a great distance away from them, even today."

"Indeed," she agreed. "But we do not need to ever return to the Sept Empire, if we choose. Nor even remain in the Free Worlds. What adventures might we have, Daniel?"

What indeed?

TWO

SHE WATCHED her personal chef turn inward, his eyes losing focus as he considered her words. From what he had said before, Kathra knew he was probably listening to the ghosts as well.

Unlike most people, Daniel's ghosts were real. Or however you might describe having a thousand other people in your head, each of whom had been a person once, a living soul, before being *taken*.

"I thought we were going to sell a few ships first?" Daniel asked tentatively.

Kathra smiled and considered the only man she could ever envision as being tough enough to belong to her comitatus.

"We are," she said simply. "But that is a means, not an end. After we find a buyer or three at Tavle Jocia, it is my hope that we have enough money to perhaps consider making larger decisions."

"Such as?"

Daniel's voice had gone just a little nervous, but he was

part of her inner council these days, with Erin and Ndidi. The ones who knew the really terrible secrets.

The dangerous ones. Secrets, as well as people.

"Commissioning more ClanStars, perhaps," she said. "Or building something to replace *WinterStar*. Perhaps an *OrchardStar*, so we can add to the gardens and trees you have aboard the Star Turtle, as well as begin growing a wider selection of things for ourselves and for trade."

He started to say something and stopped himself, just as she had known he would.

They had had this conversation many times, the two of them in private, as well as in larger groups.

He would offer her all the space currently unused on the Star Turtle he had inadvertently captured when he'd killed its owner. There were already vast orchards there, filled with many species of trees nobody had ever heard of, but which bore fruit that humans could eat safely.

She would not accept.

Daniel meant well, but to move herself and her people aboard that ship was to put all those women in a place he controlled. Daniel Lémieux was in some strange way tied to the mental powers of that gem, and became one with the Turtle when he was aboard it.

He feared turning into a Mad God at some point with all that power suddenly at his command. Daniel had confessed that to her, as well as to Ndidi, whose job it was to keep him sane.

If she could.

Areen was one woman of her crew who occasionally slept with Daniel in the physical sense, but she was also bisexual by nature, and didn't mind the touch of a male in her pleasures.

Not for Kathra, but what consenting adults did was not her problem. If Daniel could use his powers to override consent now, she wasn't worried because he had been intimate with Areen before all of this insanity began.

Daniel closed his mouth, words unspoken.

Unnecessary.

He was a smart enough person, even as a *male*, to understand that there were some lines she would never cross.

"So what do we do about my share?" he suddenly laughed. "I find it hard to envision a future where I turn the Star Turtle and those powers over to someone else and happily retire."

Kathra had to agree. The powers of Urid-Varg were gendered. Only a male could wield them, or she would have taken them for herself to protect the Mbaysey.

As well as to save Daniel from where that sort of power wanted to drag him under the surface of the water on a daily basis.

She had heard enough of those nightmares, as well.

"Do you prefer Sept Crowns or Free World Guilders?" Kathra teased the man instead. "Should we open you an account at the same bank the tribe uses?"

She caught the grimace of pain across his face before it vanished. He was one of them now.

Mbaysey.

Not all were children of the African Diaspora. Even her comitatus had *Anglos* and *Spanics* in it. Daniel was *Rabic*, ancestry from the northern coast of Africa, but radically different ethnically.

Lighter brown skin that looked more like a darkly-tanned *Anglo*. Wavy black hair instead of the tight curls of her kind. His was graying on the sides at a young age, but again, that had been occurring before, so it didn't necessarily indicate that the powers were killing him.

"If we do this," Daniel's voice turned deadly serious now,

"we might never return to even Free World space, Kathra. I might not, at least."

"Carve out your own empire in the galactic interior?" she asked.

They were alone. Ndidi wouldn't arrive to start cooking lunch for another half hour or so. That was why Kathra had come now.

Daniel's face was carved with pain. Etched with the agony of remembering himself wiping out entire species in the past. Except that had been another man, wearing his mind.

"The Sept can never understand what the Star Turtle is, Kathra," he scowled. "I am not sure if I could destroy a Septagon and get away afterwards, but they would never stop hunting me, either way. I would have to leave the Mbaysey far behind and draw the hunters after me."

"There is an alternative, if it comes to that," she countered.

"What?"

"You could destroy the Sept Empire instead."

THREE

AMIRIN PASDAR WAS AN AUSTERE MAN. In emotion. In habit. In appearance.

Even in his office, with two uncomfortable chairs facing a metal desk, with the flag of the Sept Empire on the wall behind him, where visitors would have it in their face constantly while dealing with him.

Pasdar's shaved head showed the scar that started on the left side of his forehead and ran almost all the way back, the white mark left in his dark skin when a rebel's blade had just missed penetrating his eye socket forty years ago.

In those days, Amirin Pasdar had merely been a sardar, an officer of the Emperor's Elite Forces, but already marked for greatness. He was, after all, part of the Pasdar Clan, one of the seven families that had forged the Sept Empire centuries ago.

Now he was Naupati. Commander of the great Septagon Vorgash. Perhaps he would be promoted to Argbadh soon, on his way to shah of some planet. It was possible that his career, combined with his blood, might see him as a counselor to the emperor himself, an Andarzbad, one of these days. Possibly even Anusiya, one of the *Emperor's Companions.*

Pasdar shrugged and turned his attention to the report that had finally been written up and disseminated by Septagon Uwalu. Tomorrow would take care of itself when it arrived.

He had other concerns.

The fools of the other Septagon had let the woman Omezi and her people escape them at Azgon. Not necessarily an embarrassing outcome, considering the number of Patrols, and even Septagons such as Vorgash, that had been chasing the woman and her mother for more than a decade without any success.

But that thing that came out of the depths of the gas giant itself?

Pasdar flipped the paper report sideways in order to see the image better.

The shape suggested a marine turtle, but the size comparison on the page after that gave it a length slightly greater than the seven kilometers from the bow of this very Septagon to the thruster housings rear.

The six things that looked like flippers suggested a similarity of evolution on a planet defined by a hexagonal lifeform, rather than the simple quadrupeds of Earth. It had a head that bore a remarkable resemblance to the picture of a snapping turtle included for comparison.

Scans of the vessel's interior had been ineffective. As had research to determine if there was any known species that had constructed such a machine.

What had happened immediately after these images were recorded was why a nobleman of the Sept Empire had come aboard Pasdar's vessel. A *Vuzurgan*, no less, one of the most elite of the Sept Empire itself. Not a high-ranking fleet officer at present, although Pasdar had no doubts that the man had served in his youth. But still a powerful civilian.

Only first sons of first sons wore the *Vuzurgan* title.

Pasdar finished reading the report again and confirmed that he had completely memorized it before filing it in a drawer on his side of the desk. Checking the clock, his guest would arrive in three minutes.

He stood, checked his uniform, and sat again, every bit of deep blue wool in place and spotless. Every suggestion of color was somehow muted on his uniform, compared to other men, although none would probably grasp that Pasdar had specifically instructed his tailor to adjust all the hues of fabric and thread down.

Let other men parade as peacocks. Not Amirin Pasdar.

A knock at the hatch, followed exactly two seconds later by the steel door sliding sideways just enough for an aide to look in carefully and confirm Pasdar's nod.

"Your guest arrives, Naupati," the man said, withdrawing immediately.

The door opened the rest of the way and Pasdar rose to greet Farrokh Shahin Mirzadeh, *Vuzurgan* of the Keyaksar himself, Emperor Dana Bahram Tabatabaei.

"Greetings, and well come," Pasdar inclined his head to the man. "I am honored to host you, *Vuzurgan* Mirzadeh."

They were of an age, roughly. Past the first surge of youth and foolishness, but not to the years of decline that eventually led into subsequent folly.

"The honor is mine, Naupati Pasdar," the visitor replied with a similar nod. "I come bearing news of great portent."

Pasdar nodded with a serious mien. Nothing less would bring such a man so far from the Imperial capital at Rhages.

Pasdar turned his attention to the aide, still waiting in the door for orders.

"Tea," he said, turning to his guest. "Hot or cold?"

"Cold," the man said.

Pasdar nodded and the aide closed the door to depart.

They sat in companionable silence for perhaps ten seconds when the *Vuzurgan* smiled.

"I have been instructed that you are not a man for elaborate ceremony and distractions, Naupati Pasdar," the visitor said. "So with your permission, I will skip the next thirty minutes of banality where we inquire of common relatives and recent journeys, and move to the heart of my orders, that you might more quickly begin planning your next move."

Pasdar nodded carefully. He was aware of his reputation, but perhaps he needed to cultivate a less brusque manner. It would never do to be labeled as just another thick-headed warrior when one might become a voice in the councils of Emperors.

"If you feel the situation warrants," he offered carefully, watching the man's dark eyes for a clue. "I would never suggest a deviation from proper behavior to one such as you."

They were relative strangers to one another, as far as he could remember, although at some level, all of the elders of the Sept were cousins.

Mirzadeh smiled knowingly back.

"Important people value your judgement, Pasdar," the man said. "They sent me so that I might impress upon you that this situation is being taken quite seriously at the highest levels."

Pasdar nodded silently. He had his theories, and his own spies, but much of what must have been discussed had remained in a tightly-closed circle, as nothing of note had leaked.

"The renegades who call themselves Mbaysey flaunt their independence from the Sept on a daily basis," Mirzadeh continued. "They threaten morals and social structures with their perversions as well, where only women are welcome. Or allowed to become warriors."

"True," Pasdar replied when the man stopped for an opinion. "But their ships can move faster than ours. Their lack of a logistics train frees them from dependence on any planet, so they can simply trade and move on, like the ancient horsemen of the steppes on Earth."

"Indeed," Mirzadeh acknowledged. "And eventually they would have been driven entirely into the darkness, or subjugated. Either was an acceptable outcome, which is why the Sept Fleet has never dedicated the necessary resources to hound them."

He paused, as if finding the words. Pasdar waited for the other shoe to drop.

"That is going to change," *Vuzurgan* Mirzadeh intoned severely.

FOUR

Dinner.

Ndidi had planned something simple tonight, but Daniel had finished his book translation process ahead of schedule and decided at lunch that he was going to help her, rather than mostly watching and answering questions. So she had put his *Rabic* ass to work in the kitchen to keep him busy.

It was still technically his kitchen. His job as Head Chef. But for the last month she had treated everything here as an extended job interview. From the smiles on various faces as she helped bus tables now, it had not gone unnoticed.

Ndidi Zikora might never be a warrior, flying one of the Commander's Spectre fightercraft, but she had been accepted by the comitatus as one of them otherwise, just as Daniel had. He was in the back now, cleaning and leaving her to the front.

Erin was still seated as the others departed, watching Ndidi move.

Ndidi studied the woman out of the corner of her eye, trying to gauge what thoughts she should expect.

Erinkansilemi "Erin" Uduik was the Commander's

Second. The woman who had her left hand in all things, and the one the rest of them answered to when Kathra Omezi wasn't around.

Ndidi was almost as tall as Daniel, so extremely short around here. Kathra was a whole head taller, and Erin split the difference. From what Ndidi had been taught, Erin was taller than most men by a shade, just like so much of the comitatus.

On the older woman's right cheek was a tattoo, in the ancient style of a barcode, wide and narrow vertical lines that a laser scanner could use to identify property.

Grandma Ezinne bore the original mark, from her time as a slave, before the Sept had finally stopped allowing such things. Erin had the same mark done to remind herself and everyone else that things could change back just as quickly. The leg that ended at the right knee with a mechanical replacement reminded her that she was a warrior.

The Sept Empire would eventually decide that the Mbaysey should no longer be free.

These women would die fighting such a pronouncement, and Ndidi would happily join them in battle, but she knew, as did everyone else, that there was little the Mbaysey could do to thwart the will of a distant emperor, if he chose.

Only Daniel might have that power, but Ndidi knew what it would cost him to wield it. Already, he had lost weight, planed down hard by the effort the power took. She watched him every day, as Kathra had ordered. Stuffed food in the man's mouth when he forgot to feed himself, either in the kitchen, or when he was translating dead letters for new dreamers.

Heard his secrets, perhaps the only other person besides Kathra so honored. Or so weighed down. Knew what nightmares awakened him in the darkness, even on nights that Areen might lay with him.

Ndidi would never do such a disgusting thing, but she could watch over her friend and keep him safe.

"Ndidi," Erin spoke now, drawing her eyes.

The hall was empty, the last stragglers finally departing to return to whatever it was such warrior women did when they weren't flying or training.

Erin patted the space next to her at the table, so Ndidi joined her silently, aware of secrets even Erin did not know.

"Erin," Ndidi acknowledged as she sat. "How may I be of service?"

Technically, she was not of the Commander's comitatus, although all treated her as a sister in service. Certain rules must still be obeyed.

"Big happenings are coming," Erin said cryptically, but that wasn't anything Ndidi didn't already know.

Daniel finishing his translation of the K'bari book was always going to herald a new chapter. Few knew much of the endless darkness beyond the Sept Empire, still mostly centered on Earth, or the Free Worlds, clinging to this side, where the Mbaysey Tribal Squadron generally traded.

But there were many other things out there. Places to see. People to meet. Not all of them could be counted on to be friendly, but Kathra and Daniel had plans in place.

Perhaps the Mbaysey could escape the Sept Empire forever?

Ndidi nodded to the senior woman, only a few years older than her, but still premier warrior of Kathra's elite.

"Daniel will be away as often as he is here," Erin continued.

Ndidi nodded again. All things already known and discussed. Nothing that would justify the seriousness in the woman's tone.

"I have spoken with Kathra," Erin announced in that way she did when she wanted to sound professorial.

Then she just dangled things out there silently.

Three months ago, Ndidi realized, she would be fidgeting with energy right now.

Today, she simply watched the woman. Calm. Dispassionate. Maybe even a little grown-up, although she would never admit such a thing in public. The teasing would never end.

But she saw the smile as it started in Erin's eyes, before finally emerging on her lips.

"It is time you trained the other kitchen staff to replace you as well, Ndidi Zikora," Erin said. "You'll be away with Daniel on his adventures, probably as much as I am, and we need to make sure the other women eat well."

Oh.

She would not be here to cook.

Ndidi was mentally rocked back onto her heels, but it made perfect sense. They could not take the Star Turtle to any TradeStations, lest they draw the eyes of every pirate and criminal in space, and not just the Sept watchers. Enough attention would arrive when *WinterStar* strode up with unique space ships to sell, and Daniel would have to be present to explain things to prospective buyers.

Kathra had ordered her to become his assistant, but also to become his friend.

Had she already reached a point in life where she wasn't going to be able to cook regularly?

Ndidi finally understood that wicked gleam in Erin's eyes.

And all the profanities that occasionally emerged from Daniel's mouth, at where his life choices had taken him.

FIVE

ONE OF THE fringe benefits of her rank, Erin decided as she settled into the strange flight throne of the ship, was that she got to do things like fly truly alien spaceships from time to time.

Oh certainly, Kathra occasionally pulled rank to fly them herself, but Erin got to remind the woman when she did that she was supposed to be in charge, rather than just flying around.

At least this vessel had belonged to a species distantly related to the upynth. Erect bipeds of a design close enough to human to be comparable.

Erin could only imagine trying to fly the one tucked back into a far corner of another bay. Daniel had said that the species called itself bhaorajj, but that was just another term for nightmare, as far as Erin was concerned.

Centaurs from legend, more or less. Except similar to spiders. Torso like a human, covered over with feathers, of all things. Two arms, hands, head, eyes.

It was the lower half of the body that would make flying that ship interesting. Six legs, three on a side, where the abdomen rested in a thing Daniel described as a nest and she thought of as a saddle. Six feet each independently controlling some aspect of flight.

In combat, they were probably more dangerous than the best Spectre pilot on her best day, just because they had eight limbs doing things and she only had four. Plus compound eyes, so they could see all directions.

Erin turned to Daniel, flying next to her today in the co-pilot's seat. This had become their norm in the SkyCamels, running back and forth between the Star Turtle and *WinterStar*. The upynth relatives that had once owned this ship were more her size, so he looked almost like a child, with his feet dangling slightly.

The look on his face said he knew what she was thinking, but it wouldn't be the first time she had made such a joke at his expense.

"You'd look silly with green and brown fur stripes for hiding in foliage," he smiled at her. "Even if you do have the right Mohawk going. We'd need to dye that as well. Not sure how the horn would look in the middle of your forehead."

Erin laughed out loud. He had found a picture of an upynth in a database to show her a close-enough approximation of the species that Urid-Varg had stolen this ship from. The so-called Conqueror of Known Space had been keeping a low profile at the time, so he hadn't tried taking any worlds and holding them, but that had only been a century ago, and not all that far away, as galactic distances went.

Not like the z'lud, where Urid-Varg had stayed for a millennium and only been driven from their region at the point where he had nearly wiped the entire species out.

They both sobered simultaneously, as though having the same thoughts. It was possible. She'd been inside his mind enough times.

Been him, in some bizarre way that no religion or science she knew could explain.

He had no secrets from her. Or Ndidi. Or even Kathra.

At the same time, they had none from him. It was a weird way to establish a working relationship, but they had all found their place to be comfortable with it.

Erin turned the other way and glanced far enough back to see Ndidi in a jumpseat.

"Buckled in?" she asked

"All set," came the response.

"Flight Control, this is Spectre Two," Erin called into the radio. "Departure imminent."

"All lanes clear, Spectre Two," Ife replied.

The radio traffic was a ruse. Kathra and a few other women were aft for this trip, but she couldn't just announce that over the comm. Too big of a chance that someone might attempt something stupid, even with sixteen Spectres in the sky flying escort.

Erin closed the line and opened the intercom as she began to unlock various controls.

"Leaving now," Erin announced.

WinterStar had a flight bay for SkyCamels. Like the Spectres, you flew along the bottom of the wheel to a ramp that would deploy, matching speed and vector before engaging magnets to hold you in place while the ship winched you up into a bay.

This transport had the requisite gear already built in, unlike a few of them that didn't, mostly in the older section of the captured vessels.

Launching was similar, in that the camels were lowered into space and then could launch forward or slip back, depending on the need for relative speed. The Spectres came off the frame hot.

"Daniel, how did he land things without magnets?" Erin asked suddenly, more curious than anything.

"It is a technology humans don't use, don't have, at least not yet," he replied in that voice that said he was trying to translate something into something into something into Spacer. Messy, but he was getting pretty good at it, at least with the more recent memories. "A beam of force is expanded like a spider web, capturing the vessel and pulling it or pushing it."

"Can we replicate it?" she glanced over as she asked.

He shrugged. Daniel was pretty good at that.

And it was one of the reasons so many women were willing to tolerate him. He didn't have all that testosterone demanding that he answer in the affirmative and only later admit that he'd been lying.

If Daniel didn't know, he was woman enough to say so. Saved everybody effort.

"Urid-Varg was not a technician," Daniel finally said. "Some of the men he captured were, so I know strange dreams, but none of us have really tried to dive deep into the oldest memories. Some of those folks are extremely strange creatures."

"What was Urid-Varg?" Ndidi asked now as Erin cleared the flight platform and waddled slowly away.

This ship was something a little more impressive than a transit bus, but not so interesting as a fightercraft. Maybe a yacht with a small crew. Ninety meters long and ten or twelve on the beam, it had the feeling of subdued wealth.

Erin didn't let that subtlety blind her to the fact that it was culturally unique and therefore possibly priceless in this sector of space. Alien tech could always find a rich buyer needing something special in his collection to show up a rival.

Again, the strange silence as Daniel went deep inside himself.

"Mnapyre," he said in a dark tone, pronouncing it *OOM-na-pire*. "He was the last of his kind, like a terrible wizard that has outlived all the others with his magic. Except he preyed on them as long as they lived, before moving on to others later."

"Ten thousand years ago?" Ndidi pressed.

"Maybe twelve," Daniel said. "I have not sat down and counted the years with each being. Some of them will not speak with me, while others do not know how."

That brought about an awkward silence. Twelve thousand years ago, humans were just discovering writing.

"Tavle Jocia Flight Control, this is Spectre Two on approach," Erin said to distract everyone from the sorts of morbid thoughts she knew they would be having.

The benefit, she supposed, of sharing Daniel's mind with them as a group on several occasions.

"Acknowledged, Spectre Two," the man at the other end called. "Maintain course and heading for docking. Customs officers are waiting."

Yes, they would be, wouldn't they? Nobody had ever seen anything like this ship before, and many people would want to know how and where Kathra Omezi and the Mbaysey had acquired it, especially since it was in good enough shape to fly.

SIX

DANIEL WAS NOT ALL that impressed by the Tavle Jocia TradeStation.

He knew that relating it to places like Genarde wasn't a fair comparison, but Daniel had only ever left the supposedly-safe confines of the Sept Empire after he had accepted a job offer so different from anything he ever envisioned that it had intrigued him. Even more than that month as a short order cook in a burger dive had been.

He didn't have much to compare this to, save the Sept worlds he had previously traveled.

And cooking for Kathra Omezi hadn't turned out to be anything as dreary as he had feared it might be, once upon a time. Daniel wasn't sure he would ever achieve boring again in his life. Certainly not here.

Most TradeStations in the Free Worlds were a little seedy, according to what he had seen and been told. That wasn't the case with Tavle Jocia. There was money here.

Several of the major trade routes through the Free Worlds crossed this system, bringing goods from all over space to this station, however briefly. As a result, Trade Barons, plural, thrived here.

On most stations, you might have one seriously rich merchant, and then a second tier of players. Tavle Jocia had at least five who might have been wealthy enough to afford to hire someone like Daniel Lémieux as a personal chef, at least for a little while.

He was too much of a control freak to live at someone else's beck and call for long, but he'd been wandering while he tried to figure out why he was so unhappy with life. Still wasn't sure he'd truly found it, so much as had the future thrust upon him like some heroic fool in a fairy tale.

But it allowed Kathra to take her team out to a nice dinner on the station, in a place that might have vied for their own Golden Diamond from Gastropode magazine, were they several thousand light-years closer to Earth, and all the politics that wrapped themselves around *that* level of snobbery.

Briefly, as the maître d' sat them, Daniel wondered if he should take up a part-time career as a field researcher, sending anonymous letters to the magazine suggesting they send folks to various places to see for themselves.

"What's so funny?" Kathra asked, primly studying his face from directly across.

He had Ndidi on his right and Erin on his left, close enough that she occasionally tapped his knee with her mechanical leg when she shifted. Areen, Kathra, and Iruoma sat across from him.

"Wondering if I should take up a career as a secret agent food reporter," he murmured back.

Daniel didn't dare say that too loudly, or someone might take him seriously. Worse, they might ask who he was and then get silly if they'd heard him.

"You've already been busy enough," Kathra smiled. "If

you decide to do more, I'm not sure when you'll sleep. And I'll have to hire a whole other team just to keep up with you."

"*Bon*," he grinned. "I am probably causing enough trouble as is."

"You saved all our lives," Iruoma spoke up.

She had been there at the first, when he met Joane and Erin on that first platform. She still rose early every morning to shave her head gleaming enough to show off the complex symbols tattooed into her skull, but her fierceness was aimed outwards now.

She considered him just another woman.

"And you have all saved mine, so I think we're more or less even," he replied.

She smiled back at him and conversation stalled as they turned to the menus.

Eating in a restaurant was a rare treat, even for most of the comitatus. They usually ate whatever was in the kitchen, which, before Daniel had come along, had been generally pedestrian at best.

Even today, Erin usually flew SkyCamels to TradeStations because that let her see the local color and enjoy the local food. Daniel frequently joined her simply to see what inspiration he might derive.

It was one thing to know ten thousand recipes. It was another to remember to cycle beyond the hundred or so at the top of his mind.

Dinner itself proved to be exceptional. Kathra was treating everyone to something nice, so they all had splurged for the sorts of prime cut steaks that they would never do on the ship, where food needed to stretch as far as possible.

The dessert choices were wider than he would normally make for a single meal, but not really as good. Industrially-well-made, he supposed.

Certainly lacking art. But it was a restaurant, and the

steaks had been exceptional, so he was willing to cut them some slack, but only after he had tried a single bite from each of the four things the others had ordered and were sharing.

"Now what?" he asked the Commander as they rose and began to make their way to the front door.

Something pulled him up so short that Ndidi plowed into him from behind.

It was most fulfilling, a second later, to be surrounded by women warriors with pistols drawn and facing out, even in the nicest restaurant on a nice station. Nobody took their own security for granted.

"Daniel?" Kathra asked in a tight, quiet voice.

"There," he said, suddenly running hell for leather down a corridor for reasons he could not fathom, let alone explain.

Out the door and turn right. The crowd was not terrible, as stations never really went to sleep at night, but the mob wasn't so bad that he couldn't move quickly.

Nobody stood out as he raced. Many people, apparently innocently, walked away from him, so he could not tell what it was that drew him, except that something had *touched* him as he stood to leave the restaurant.

And it had been external. The voices in his head had more or less worked out a method of drawing his attention when they wanted something. They weren't ghosts, but maybe the echoes of ghosts, so they would respond to tell him something he needed to know, rather than complain for the sake of complaining.

But the touch had been similar.

It was gone now.

Only Erin made any sound when she ran, but that was because she hadn't bothered with the matching boot she sometimes wore. At least she had worn longer pants today, so her mechanical knee and shin weren't obvious most of the time, except she thumped the deck with her leather-covered heel, pounding in his wake.

At the curve, he gave up. Slowed to a stop, pivoted in place, and studied everyone around him with the mental sight he had stolen from Urid-Varg when he killed the *salaud*.

Most of the faces turned his way were *tsk*ing in their heads at his behavior, but nobody broadcast any sort of emotion that they had been watching him. That they had touched him.

But somebody had.

Daniel realized that he wasn't even breathing heavy from the run. None of the women were, either, but they were all warriors, including Ndidi, who was technically just another cook like him. He had gotten in much better shape.

Kathra grabbed his sleeve and tugged him out of the middle of the concourse to a quiet corner, holstering her pistol while the others kept watch.

"Immediate threat?" she asked in a quiet, simple tone.

Daniel closed his eyes and looked around once more, just to be sure.

"No," he said, opening them. "It's gone now."

"Explain later," Kathra said. "Everyone relax and pretend like nothing happened."

The other women straightened up and weapons vanished in the blink of an eye.

Kathra studied his face for a long moment, as if committing something to memory, and then pulled out her skyvox. Quickly, she checked something and then began to walk.

Everyone fell in behind her, but Daniel noted that both Ndidi and Erin were beside him and Areen and Iruoma walked several paces behind him, rather than ahead.

Whatever it was, they were all taking it seriously.

Kathra led them out of the tourist area of the TradeStation to a lift in a quiet side corridor. She pressed the button, waited a moment, and then spoke.

"Kathra Omezi to see Factor Isaev," she said into the microphone.

The door slid open and she entered. Daniel knew a long moment of doubt before he could make his legs work, but this lift didn't appear to be a trap.

Whoever it had been earlier was hopefully just watching, for now.

But how had they managed to hide from him?

SEVEN

THE LIFT DOORS closed and Kathra found herself and her cook surrounded by a team of high-strung killers, intent on doing violence for her at the drop of a hat right now. Whatever had infected Daniel had spread to the other women. However, she didn't have his story yet, and this open deck wasn't the place to have that kind of discussion.

Rather than speak, Kathra reached out a hand and pulled Areen to one side and behind her, instead of standing right in front of the doors and prepared to take a beam from someone when they opened.

She caught Daniel's eye and his nod. Anyone attempting violence now would have to deal with him, and he was at least as rattled, perhaps as angry, as he had been while fleeing Azgon, from the stories he and Ndidi had shared after their escape.

But she could relax. After all, the Factor himself had invited her, intent on possibly expanding his collection of exotic vessels, if the price was right.

He would make no untoward moves this early in the relationship. Not the least because her message had mentioned that this was just the *first* such vessel coming onto the market, and not even the most interesting.

That should pique anybody's interest. The Mbaysey had a reputation, as far as she knew, as a poor tribe that mined for metals and exotic gases, trading them at various stations for food and electronics that they could not make themselves.

Nowhere was there a history of owning a junkyard filled with old, valuable starships.

Something must have happened…

And the stories would be even stranger when she started selling some of the truly alien craft she had inherited.

The lift doors opened onto a chamber that could only be described as lush. Carpeting thick enough under her feet that she didn't hear footsteps. Overstuffed chairs in two corners that looked deep enough to fall into and never escape. Harder chairs on the other side for people who didn't need as much decadence.

The strangest thing for her was the fish tank taking up an entire side wall of the chamber. One meter thick, running three meters to the ceiling and wall to wall across the six meter room. Because she owned the two *WaterStars*, both filled with a variety of fish to feed her tribe, she recognized a few of the species in here, but not many.

Daniel might do a little better, but she was willing to bet that even he got lost before he reached halfway.

Before they got settled, or distracted by the fish, a door opened in the far wall. The man who entered had the look of a majordomo. A gray-haired, senior servant to a powerful man, who was still probably a power in his own right.

He certainly smelled like it, with an expensive perfume about him that was industrial chemicals in origin, rather than the sort of plant oils some of her ClanStars produced for trade.

"Commander Omezi," he said with the faintest nod as she turned to him. "The Factor will see you now."

She gestured for the others to find seats or get comfortable and nodded at Daniel to join her. The newcomer looked like he wanted to say something.

"My mechanic will be necessary," she smiled down at the tiny *male*, barely any taller than her cook. "He fully understands the technology involved, and will be the only one able to explain it to your specialists. You did bring stellar architects, yes?"

The man's face soured for the briefest moment. Probably didn't have any on staff, and had been forced to hire some for the occasion. Or better, was expecting any of the mechanics he did have on staff would be good enough and was possibly rethinking that decision at the last moment.

The man retreated, rather than try to match wills with her. Kathra followed him deeper into the suite, glancing once to make sure Daniel was with her.

On top of everything else, his mental powers made him the best bodyguard she could ever conceive of having right now, even before his paranoia got ramped up.

Down a hall, they entered a different wing of the abode, and passed through a large space that felt more like the salon where favorites and powerful guests were entertained. Still decorated using a stupendous amount of Free World Guilders, but done tastefully.

Money showing off, but being a little more polite about it.

Kathra Omezi had never had money. The Mbaysey produced significant budgets, but every Crown and Guilder went into operating costs and repairs, with very little left over merely for decorating a room.

The majordomo led them to a door and stepped to one side.

Kathra had seen a variety of pictures of the Trade Factor. Mikhail Isaev was a tall, bulky man, standing on the far side of an ornate, wooden desk. Nearly her height, but at least fifty kilograms heavier, and very little of that was muscle.

Most of the images had been manipulated to show the man off better.

The hair on his head was artificial. She could see the seam, three centimeters above his ears, where the last of his natural stuff had been dyed recently, but faded from matching the fibers higher up. The tan was fake as well, but that looked like chemicals the man ate with his breakfast, rather than a cream he slathered on his skin. Too orange for someone who had to stand under a tanning light in the shower, as most *Anglos* like Isaev did. Daniel didn't require as much, but still some.

Kathra was already almost the color of night, so the tanning for her was just the vitamins and benefits of sunlight, for a woman who never set foot on an actual planet unless she had to.

"Welcome," he said in a voice almost as fake as the rest of him.

Still, this man represented the opportunity for a surge of wealth that might even break the chains that bound her to the Free Worlds, even as she had already decided that she would never return to a Sept TradeStation.

At least not without riding in the head of Daniel's Star Turtle, intent on doing some level of violence.

Kathra sat and studied the scene as the two men joined her. Daniel was keyed up from whatever he had seen or sensed in the restaurant. Isaev was more naturally paranoid, from the look of him.

They made small talk for the requisite period of time, Daniel remaining mum and allowing her to field all questions, in spite of the occasional glances thrown his way.

If you didn't know who he was already, I'm not going to tell you know, Factor Isaev.

"So I am given to understand from our earlier communications that the vessel you have currently for sale is unique, and part of a larger set?" he asked finally, stepping to business rather than discussing opera seasons and other frivolities any longer.

"Unique, yes," she agreed. "I would only classify it as part of a larger set in the sense that we have had the opportunity to salvage a number of vessels from where they have been stored for some time, and sell them on the private market."

"And where did they originate?" Isaev asked, focusing what Kathra supposed was meant to be charisma on her.

It might work with a woman whose stomach wasn't turned by the thought of being touched by a *male*. Even Daniel would not rate highly, although she had had the occasional thought to explore the sorts of orgasms he might induce with his mental powers, were she to ask.

"From a number of places," Kathra smiled and deflected the question. No use explaining any more than utterly necessary. "The prior owner was controlled by a larger conglomerate that is no longer a viable business concern. The successor-in-interest contacted me about marketing and disposing of the vessels."

"Successor-in-interest?" Isaev turned savvy.

Probably surprised that a poor tribal woman like her understood the term.

That the Free Worlds wasn't as racist or sexist as the Sept Empire wasn't a particularly high bar to clear, and an entire tribal nation ruled by Central African Diaspora women was probably utterly exotic to the man.

"Myself," Daniel spoke up, using a dry, superior tone that suggested he might be wealthy enough to buy this station if he chose. "Through the vagaries of inheritance, I now own the entire collection, and have no interest in it whatsoever, either to maintain, or to even own. Thus I have retained the Commander to handle the chore."

She liked the way Daniel stared at the man for a long beat before continuing.

"That and the fact that some of these craft apparently represent manufacturing technologies that neither the Free Worlds nor the Sept can currently replicate," Daniel smiled. "My predecessors preferred alien technologies wherever possible. Some of them I cannot sell off because they are immobile in their current location and I have no interest in letting those coordinates be known, lest pirates decide to become involved."

"They are at risk?" Isaev asked, perking up.

"I would prefer not to annihilate any more fools, going forward," Daniel replied evenly. "Even pirates who probably have it coming."

Kathra held the chuckle deep in her stomach, lest Isaev think she was mocking him.

Daniel had only killed one person, as far as she knew. But Urid-Varg might have been the worst xenocide in history, if even a portion of the stories were true.

"So the price you listed for the ship is merely a guess?" Isaev asked after nearly swallowing his tongue.

"The ship is unique in this sector of space," Kathra countered. "Research we have done suggests that it was manufactured some one hundred and fifty to two hundred years ago, roughly seven hundred to a thousand light-years spinward and closer to the galactic core, by a species that may or may not be related to the upynth, either as an offshoot or via convergent evolution."

"And it flies?" the man breathed as Kathra set the hook and slowly began to reel.

"We brought it aboard station from *WinterStar* to

demonstrate that, Factor Isaev," she said. "There are three others aboard my ship at present, which will also go onto the auction block at some point, but we decided to set a relatively low price for this ship up front, as a way of demonstrating to the Free Worlds what value we have."

"And you contacted me directly, rather than auctioning this one?" he asked, suddenly suspicious.

Gift horses, and all that.

"You have a reputation as a collector, Factor," she smiled primly. "The other individuals we might have talked to merely had money, and perhaps a willingness to joust with you at an auction just to make you pay more for something they didn't really desire."

He paused, studying her much more closely, Daniel almost forgotten. Possibly seeing her as more of an equal now, and not just a peasant arrived hat in hand to ask a favor.

Commander Omezi was offering a favor, instead. There was power in that sort of role reversal, and he had only just grasped that.

Men and their vanities. But then, fake hair, fake tan, fake smile.

Only the enormous wealth was real.

"What do you really want?" he finally asked, having processed any number of alternatives as she watched his eyes.

"Freedom," Daniel spoke up, further roiling the waters. "My new partners are willing to explore deep into the galactic interior for some reasons I wish to pursue, but that will be an expensive proposition. I have a collection of ships that do not interest me. Converting them to cash, or other possibilities frees me up to pursue my mission."

"Other possibilities?" he asked, perhaps missing Daniel's reference to *new partners*.

Daniel turned to Kathra now and smiled, ceding the conversation again after disturbing Isaev.

She wondered how closely he was reading the man, and if it was within Daniel's ethics right now to make adjustments to the mind of Mikhail Isaev that left him more interested in doing a deal. It might even be possible to twist the stranger hard enough to make him sign anything, but she knew Daniel would see that as the left hand of evil.

It was no more acceptable to do those things to a woman than they were to a man, but Daniel might see a wedge of daylight there, with a cut-throat businessman who might already be planning to cheat them later.

Just another reason she had brought him.

"We need the ability to travel far from friendly TradeStations, Factor," Kathra said. "Most of my ships are self-sufficient as a tribal squadron, but we would like to explore the possibility of commissioning some new designs."

"And I own the largest ships foundry in the sector," he smiled at her, suddenly understanding. "The level of trust between the two of you appears impressive, Commander."

"It is."

She smiled, understanding that he would, of course, try to break that bond later, never considering that she had been inside Daniel's mind, and he in hers, to know how they must pursue this mission.

Daniel didn't want to go back to the Sept Empire. Might never be able to, unless he could convince those officials that he didn't know anything useful from his time traveling with them, when the Sept Fleet seemed intent on chasing her.

But he also had a Star Turtle that would need to be dealt with. Somehow.

And all the potential to turn into a Mad God that came with it.

"So you wish to sell this one vessel for cash?" Isaev said, leaning back and *calculating* angles. "And then, having attracted my attention, possibly do a private deal for the rest, with payment in upgrades and new tonnage for your squadron?"

"It will be a long, dangerous journey, to see things no human alive has ever witnessed, Factor," Kathra said. "We need to talk about commissioning a warship."

EIGHT

Amirin Pasdar would still be a naupati in command, at least on paper. He would continue to command Septagon Vorgash, but he would do so in a different manner than he had before.

Looking around his office, nothing had changed. And yet, everything had.

The Great Ships, for all their terrible firepower, were essentially defensive weapons, even on the attack. You parked in orbit of a planet you wished to control, and allowed the Axial Megacannon to simply awe them into submission, perhaps after destroying a city or two from orbit if they chose to resist, just to make your point.

He could not chase down a fleeing vessel, as speed on the valence drives was a factor of the same mass that made a Septagon such a dangerous weapon. And the Patrols that fanned out like wolfpacks could only drive off the pirates, calling in the Fleet once such a world as hosted them had been identified.

Pasdar could not do that here.

The Mbaysey were not tied to a single star system. They

could mine the resources they generally needed from any average solar system, crushing up asteroids and small moons for solids, and finding water in the frozen depths. Any sufficiently-large gas or ice giant and patience would see them most of the trace gases they needed as well.

Only bulk production of food and advanced electronics prevented them from leaving human space forever.

So Pasdar was functionally promoted to argbadh now, commanding a flotilla of vessels, rather than just the Septagon around him and the usual two Patrols of smaller craft that he could use as scouts. He would need half a dozen Patrols on this mission. That required the attachment of over fifty other vessels to his normal force, just to supply the food, fuel, and supplies that four hundred thousand soldiers and support staff consumed on any given day.

Squadrons of cargo vessels would fly to and fro regularly. Those would require escorts, bases, resupply of their own.

He felt like an ancient general, planning a campaign of conquest down off the Persian plateau in pursuit of one of the ancient mobs of horsemen that had once run wild across the grasslands of the north.

Pasdar had studied his enemy in preparation for this mission almost as closely as he had studied the history of such things. They were almost never successful.

Instead, some would-be conqueror would build a fort or two at a spot and the barbarians would simply ride out of sight rather than offering battle. After enough time, such large armies would have to march somewhere else to put down uprisings or conquer other cities, leaving the new city weak.

The barbarians, depending, could then either demand trade, or simply sack the place, if they chose. In many instances, trade had been more dangerous over the long term, because the merchants then began to demand more trade and less taxes.

Unless you successfully built a sophisticated bureaucracy, empires built on the personality of one man were like sand castles, rising in the morning but gone when the afternoon tide returned.

Amirin Pasdar was not trying to conquer new domains for his emperor to try and hold. No, he was only to pursue the woman. That much had been communicated to him by the *Vuzurgan* himself.

Kathra Omezi was a footnote, as far as Pasdar was really concerned. The entire Mbaysey tribe were just minor rebels that had never been important enough to deal with, and even today had not risen to that level.

But she had found allies. Powerful, unknown, obviously alien. Before their spy had been discovered and presumably executed, they had been told that they would find something at Azgon. Something magical, and equally dangerous.

Septagon Uwalu had found a turtle. One capable of shrugging off Ram Cannon fire. And smart enough to dodge the terrible beam of the Axial Megacannon.

But then it had done…something.

Reports were generally consistent enough to be accepted as truth, as much truth as the soldiers interviewed were capable of explaining. A primal scream that everyone on the vessel seemed to hear at the same instant.

Rage so great that power systems and computers failed and rebooted themselves, rendering all sensor data broken and suspect.

And then, one final message communicated: *You will never catch me.*

Pasdar's orders stated that he didn't need to catch this creature, whoever he was. Pasdar only needed to pursue him. Identify him as a species and a location.

Determine if the Sept Fleet should return with an entire battle squadron of Septagons, something they had not formed in decades, in order to eliminate any threat posed by that vessel and its ilk, as it knew enough to fear the Axial Megacannon.

What could an entire squadron do?

Pasdar nodded to himself, alone in his office, and rose.

Exiting, he crossed the many corridors to the Command Node of the great vessel, the place where twenty men commanded the one thousand who in turn led three hundred thousand.

Troopers only registered his progress by opening hatchways as he approached, closing them after he passed. One of them would notify the Node that he was coming, but they should already expect that, as he was only four minutes early for the shift he had scheduled.

Was it excitement that drove him?

That itself was an interesting datum to consider. Was the thrill of the hunt capable of changing him from who he had been into someone new? Amirin Pasdar had no doubt that he would need to think in new patterns in order to deal with Kathra Omezi as well as to understand her new ally.

Perhaps he would indeed need to become a new person in order to succeed where he and others had failed. Perhaps others had chased her with classical Sept rules that she knew as well as they did, and thus were always destined to failure?

Pasdar made a note to meditate on the concept during his next rest period.

He entered the Command Node via the Great Causeway, taking in the whole of the horseshoe-shaped bridge at a glance. Below him was a deck as he walked, two groups of officers seated in semi-darkness under his balcony, with oversized screens set so that he could walk over and stand above an officer should he choose. Thus the twenty were always at hand to take his orders.

His aspbad was on duty today, rather than one of his marzbans, as this would be a momentous event. Hadi Rostami rose from his lesser command chair as Pasdar entered and turned to face his commander.

Technically, even a vessel as large as a Septagon was only under the command of an aspbad, just as Patrol squadrons were. The naupati commanded the entire force, but he did so from an aspbad's deck.

Pasdar had selected Rostami personally, after his predecessor had retired. Although he was named for a great warrior from history, this descendent was more of a scholar, tall and skinny, compared to Pasdar's own powerful build. It was his mind that Pasdar required, as Hadi Rostami was one of the most intelligent men Amirin had ever met, capable of tracking an impossible number of threads and details simultaneously as Pasdar needed them.

The man came to attention and smiled silently.

Pasdar smiled back. He studied the backs of heads below him, and the few screens he could see, but the lower deck was generally in shadows.

"Status?" Pasdar asked simply as he came to rest in front of the man, both of them standing in front of the Command Thrones from which they controlled their respective charges.

"All vessels ready for departure, Naupati," Rostami replied quietly, proudly, for his name would share some of the glory of this mission. "Two staging depots have been established forward for rendezvous and are awaiting further orders."

Pasdar took a deep breath and considered the endless darkness out the bow of Septagon Vorgash, those unknown seas he must sail on the greatest voyage of exploration in more than a century.

He would make his name, either as a hero or a fool. Thus had the elders of the Empire chosen him.

Amirin Pasdar would ensure that his name was never forgotten.

"All vessels transition to valence drives," he ordered.

History awaited.

NINE

Daniel's head hurt, but a glass of wine was helping grind that sharp edge down to a duller one right now. Still, he had been focused on that Trade Factor long enough to have left a sour, dirty taste in his mouth.

Some of Kathra's good Malbec was the cure.

They had flown back to *WinterStar* after the meeting, the comitatus again scrambled and flying escort, since it would be generally known that the Commander was aboard the strange craft. Nobody had bothered them, and *WinterStar* had withdrawn to a distance Kathra had considered safe.

Daniel would have liked to have brought the Turtle with them, but he understood the need to hide it from prying eyes. He just had to remember not to become psychologically dependent on the craft.

He was alone in his quarters with the bottle, having had enough of everyone else, thank you very much, so the knock at the hatch was not particularly welcome. He considered reaching out with his mind to see who it was, but that sounded like even more work than just opening the damned thing with the switch by his bed. There were only so many people it might be.

The Commander entered and closed the hatch, so he would have been right on his second guess and Daniel considered that a win here.

At least she caught him drinking alone with a glass, rather than straight from the bottle.

Daniel looked around his chambers and sighed. He rarely spent time here, except to sleep, so it was still as impersonal as the day he moved in nearly a year ago. No art. No collections of gadgets, like most people accumulate. Just a bed, a chair, an end table, and a footlocker for his clothes.

He was seated on the bed. Kathra took the chair.

"Would you prefer the glass or the bottle?" he asked as she settled herself.

"That bad?" she asked.

Daniel handed her the half-full glass.

"Mikhail Isaev is a shit of the first order, Commander," Daniel said. "Reading the man like an open book just meant that I knew where to apply pressure and how to do it effectively. He'd still cheat you in a moment if he thought he could."

"What happened at the restaurant?"

"There was someone," he replied, feeling a cold spike of *something* go through him at the memory. "They had something similar to the gem that I inherited from Urid-Varg, but much less powerful. They touched me briefly, almost as if confirming who I was, and then retreated from my power before I could find them again."

"Another Mnapyre?" She took a sip, mostly companionably it seemed, rather than striving to get as drunk as he was aiming for.

"There are no more," Daniel said decisively. "I killed the last of them."

"As far as he knew," she corrected.

"As far as he knew, yes," Daniel agreed. "But he had outlived his species by several millennia, so I think it must be someone else."

"Who?"

Daniel took a long pull from the bottle and let the warm redness tamp down the jolt of fear that wanted to run through his body like electricity.

"I have only his ghosts," Daniel began. "You killed the thing that had his mental matrix inscribed on it, so I cannot tap his memories, except as they were somehow shared with his victims."

"And?"

She sipped.

"I think he was fleeing from someone," Daniel said. "The z'lud are the key."

"How so?" she leaned forward and focused those dark, deadly eyes on his flesh.

"He ruled them for centuries," Daniel said. "Destroyed them as a nation, effectively, some five or six thousand years ago. After that, he never tried to take over an entire nation and rule it for a long time. He might stay for a time, looting and doing whatever sordid things caught his fancy, but then he would move on again. Not until he got to the K'bari did he try, and that blew up eventually, too."

"Someone was chasing him?" she leaned forward, brow furrowed. The patterns buzzed into her short hair were distracting enough to catch his eye for a moment, before he pulled things back down to her face.

"Quite possibly, yes," Daniel nodded. "Who, or for what reason eludes me, but it is probably a thing to consider, going forward. You are probably at risk, though."

"How so?" she inquired.

"If they sought to located Urid-Varg, and have begun

tracking me, then it is entirely possibly that they consider themselves powerful enough to take on the Turtle," Daniel drank some more wine to calm his suddenly racing nerves. "*WinterStar* would be no match for someone like that."

"We can always flee," Kathra sought to reassure him.

"Do not let any alien ship get close to you, Commander," Daniel said. "If they have a spider web device, I do not know how long its reach might be. *WinterStar* might become a fly."

"Noted," she said, handing him back the glass. "I will leave you to your wine now. You appear to be safe enough, but let me know if they touch you again, so we can track them instead."

"*Oui*," he nodded wearily.

A knock at the hatch distracted both of them.

For the briefest moment, Daniel panicked clear to the bottom of his soul and reached out with his powers, adrenaline surging through his entire body to the point he thought he might become physically ill.

The touch outside was warm and friendly. Patient, even.

He opened the hatch.

"Hello, Areen," he smiled at her.

That she occasionally spent the night down in his quarters was well known, but such events were not all that common. Still, she flushed like a teenager caught by her parents when she saw Kathra already standing and moving towards the door.

The Commander just laughed.

"You'll be good for what ails him," Kathra said as she reached the other woman. "Daniel is feeling small and alone tonight."

She turned from the hallway and smiled at him.

"All I need is a little time," the Commander said. "And then we might give anyone a good game."

"That's what frightens me," Daniel murmured, but she

was already departing and Areen was stuck halfway into his cabin.

"Would you like some company?" she asked in that rich alto tone of hers.

He watched her cornrow braids move as she walked, mesmerized as if by Medusa coming for him.

Her skin reminded Daniel of an old, copper Half-Crown. Not the brighter red of a new coin, but an older one that had been out in the galaxy for a while and picked up some dirt and weathering. The kind you could clean up with enough patience and the right touch.

If she allowed it.

"I can think of nothing better in this galaxy right now," Daniel replied, frozen in place.

The woman had half a head on him, and outweighed him to boot, but tonight she had turned off all the signals of the bad-ass warrior, and turned herself into a woman. Soft, pliant, gentle even.

She took the bottle from his hand and placed it carefully on the end table.

He watched, in awe as always, as she reached down and pulled her shirt over her head and tossed it onto the chair with a wry smile.

"I might have needs as well," she said, pushing him down onto his back and climbing onto the bed with him like a snake seeking warmth.

She kissed him. Daniel almost felt like a bystander, watching everything from outside his own body, but her warmth suddenly cut through the cold that had gripped his soul. He reached for her and she was there.

TEN

Kathra looked up as Erin knocked on the door frame then entered, throwing herself more or less into one of the two chairs.

"You rang?" Erin asked.

Kathra studied her second in command for a moment, closing the screen she had been reading and leaving the inventory for later. Paperwork never ended, even when you were poor.

In fact, it got more important, since every Guilder had to be accounted for, planned for, and used to the best efficiency.

"I was just down talking to Daniel," Kathra said.

Erin snorted.

"Did you manage to pry the bottle out of his hands first?" she laughed. "He looked like he needed a stiff drink by the time we got back to the ship."

"I did not, but I did drink a little with him," Kathra said. "He's in good hands now."

"Oh?" Erin sat up a little straighter.

"Areen decided to keep him company."

Kathra noted the shiver of disgust that ran through Erin's

frame. She didn't feel the same level of revulsion that a male might touch her, but she also understood that human sexuality ran along a variety of axes. Areen's bisexuality wasn't even one end, according to scientists, but it represented one end here, where few men were allowed, and most women were happy to do without their services.

She could keep the tribe intact from the refrigerator for decades right now. In fact, she would need to make such a medical visit at some point, but it could wait another year, she thought.

Erin only touched women. And that was fine. Daniel's needs were few and rather vanilla. And Areen seemed to enjoy it, so he could remain among them.

"So what did you learn from our cook?" Erin asked as she settled herself again.

"He thinks that he may be being chased," Kathra said.

"By?"

"Enemies of Urid-Varg," Kathra contemplated who such people might be, but had no answers. "People who might have been hounding that *salaud* across the galaxy and driving him into human space."

"So, dangerous?" Erin perked up, always the warrior.

"Dangerous to Urid-Varg," Kathra corrected her. "Since Daniel is in command now, they might be amenable to reason."

"Do we know anything?" Erin asked.

"Pure speculation on his part," Kathra offered. "Extrapolated outwards from the simple fact of someone touching him mentally and then retreating."

"So it could be anyone?" Erin asked.

"Someone alien, yes," Kathra agreed. "Pay attention to any non-humans you encounter on station. Anyone that seems to be too interested in our comings and goings."

"It's the Free Worlds, Kathra," Erin pointed out. "We're

not in the Sept, where ninety-five percent of the population is human. Tavle Jocia sits on so many trade routes, so far from Earth itself, that we're probably only fifty percent human on the concourse."

"Understood, but you'll make a point of traveling only in roving packs of three or more," Kathra ordered. "Armed at all times. Paranoid at all times. I'm not sure if having Daniel with us when we're on station is a good idea or a bad one, but we'll deal with that later. You inform the comitatus."

"What about recruiting?" Erin asked, her voice turning sharp.

"What about it?" Kathra countered.

"You're looking to build a bigger vessel than *WinterStar*," Erin noted. "Either we decommission our old boat, or we'll need to expand to a second crew. Same if you end up building some of the support vessels you talked about with Factor Isaev. That means vetting. If we're paranoid, do we trust anybody?"

"We have Daniel to help," Kathra's voice turned dark. "Any spies will either be deflected before they join, or we can deal with them later."

"You thinking of having Daniel turn them inside out?" Erin's eyes squinted.

"I doubt he would agree," Kathra said. "That boy is too squeamish for that, but he makes up for it elsewhere. I'll ask if it comes down to the perfect situation, but more likely we'd just execute anyone that managed to get past his abilities and your paranoia to make it aboard the squadron. And we can hold each of the ClanStars personally responsible for any spies that they recruit as we expand, so they'll be extra vigilant."

Erin nodded, but Kathra could see the way she was biting her upper lip in thought.

"Out with it," she continued.

"What about recruiting aliens?" Erin said. "Alien women, if we can identify them, following the same rules as the rest of the Mbaysey. Dare we trust them?"

Kathra leaned back in her chair and thought about it. She'd always entertained the notion, but up until now, all of her followers were human. Most of them refugees from the Sept Empire, although a few Free Worlders had joined. Usually, those were escaping bad marital situations or running away from home to prevent an arranged marriage.

They had never been this far from the Sept Empire, geographically or culturally. Or this deep in the Free Worlds, where non-humans started to become the dominant population.

The risks would go through the roof, but Mbaysey was a state of mind, not a fact of biology. Women freed from the tyranny of the racist, sexist Persians that had founded the Sept Empire. Few men allowed, and those vetted closely. All the important jobs held by women, with the sole exception of cooking for Kathra's comitatus, and even then, Ndidi was handling that chore more than Daniel.

And both would have to give way soon. Such was the nature of this adventure.

"In small groups," Kathra decided. "Individuals who walk in will be subject to the same sorts of scrutiny as mobs volunteering. And Daniel will have to meet them all. Same for the ClanStars, so we can make sure they can't communicate home."

"How would you send a message FTL?" Erin goggled and sat up.

"I have no idea, Erin," Kathra said. "But we're moving into alien realms. What can they do?"

"Point taken," Erin sat back. "Nobody can explain Daniel or the Star Turtle, either."

Erin paused, contemplative again. Kathra waited for her to decide to speak.

"Are we really considering turning our back on human space altogether?" she finally asked.

"No," Kathra said simply. "We are, however, going to see about opening new trade and communication routes to places humans have perhaps never gone, so that we might partake of their technology and at the same time not be dependent on the Free Worlds resisting the Sept Empire for our own freedom."

"You think the Sept are coming?" Erin asked.

"I have no doubts, Erin," Kathra said. "The only question in my mind is when."

ELEVEN

Tavle Jocia TradeStation. Daniel couldn't help but study the looming mass as Erin's SkyCamel was on final approach. Couldn't help but to reach out and try to smell the scents that the station gave off. The people gave off.

Whatever he had sensed a week ago was gone now. Daniel sometimes questioned his own sanity on the topic, wondering if he had imagined everything, the underlying paranoias of Urid-Varg flavoring everything.

It was not a good way to live.

He had given up wine altogether, afraid that he would slip into a bottle one of these days and never find his way out again. It was a common enough problem in a commercial kitchen, where the easiest way to deal with everyday stress involved taking a drink of something to numb the pain.

Followed by another.

And more.

"You breathing over there?" Erin asked, her voice intruding on Daniel and breaking him out of the cycle of squirreling in on himself.

Merde, he was having a bad day.

"Trying," Daniel answered.

It was always easier to simply be honest with these women. They had all seen the insides of his mind enough times to understand the truth and not be offended by it.

"Try harder," she smiled as he looked over.

That brought a smile to his face. Erin had been the hardest of the women when he first came aboard. The one most offended that Kathra had hired a *male*, and a *Rabic* one to boot.

At least he had won her over.

"So we have time before the meeting," Daniel said. "What's on the afternoon schedule?"

"K'bari," Erin replied, her grin growing even wider.

"Huh?"

Daniel was feeling especially eloquent today.

"That book you found on K'bari history was hidden in a Sept cookbook," she said, turning a little more serious now. "We have time to haunt Tavle Jocia's darker corners and see if there's anything interesting. Remember where we're likely to go next, if all this works out."

"I feel like the child in the fairy tale," Daniel sobered. "Following a trail of breadcrumbs backwards in the forest, waiting for the evil witch that my grandmother warned me about."

"Fortunately, you brought along all the big, bad wolves, Daniel," Erin laughed. "We'll protect you."

"That you'll even need to is my fear, Erin," he replied. "I'd rather just stay in my kitchen and commit art, but then I'm in Ndidi's hair all the time as well."

"What are you two talking about?" her voice floated up from the rear. "I heard my name."

"The need to teach you small arms and close combat, Ndidi," Erin called back.

"I can dice some fool just as well as I can a tomato," Ndidi sassed.

Daniel turned in his chair by loosening his harness a little. The SkyCamel wasn't carrying any cargo today, and the alien ship was currently docked aboard *WinterStar* while Kathra worked out her deal with the Trade Factor. Ndidi, Joane, and Iruoma were strapped in back there, waiting to get to the station and go for a walk.

Kathra had ordered three, so Erin had brought three with her when she and Daniel went to the station. He certainly felt more secure than he would have alone, with these women around him, but it didn't help but give him a terrible foreboding as well.

"Stand by for docking," Erin called to everyone.

The SkyCamel entered the maw of the landing bay like a great whale swallowing them, and then they were committed as the mouth closed.

Slowly, the side walls moved in and locked into place to provide the smallest volume that needed to be pressurized, and air began to hiss against the hull.

Daniel felt the band around his chest loosening as the air pressure built up around them. He unbuckled last and stood, moving to the rear of the shuttle and waiting for the door to open.

Out onto the concourse, he sniffed, but didn't detect evil or malignancy aimed at him or the women surrounding him. Hopefully, there was none.

And if you believed that, I've got a used starship to sell you.

Except that he did have used ships to sell people, so maybe that was a bad metaphor. Some of them were so alien that they didn't even use valance drives to move between stars, so he couldn't sell them until Kathra Omezi figured out their secrets.

What was an entirely new stardrive technology worth on the open market?

"You okay?" Ndidi stepped close and stared into his eyes.

"Define *okay*," he smiled at her grimly. "I successfully managed pants this morning, against great odds. Presumably we'll be eating lunch in public at some point and I shall strive not to embarrass the rest of you. Am I wound too tight for my own good? Oh, *oui*."

"As long as you've got it under control," Ndidi grinned at him and turned in such a way that she could lean in with her shoulder and bump him.

It was a friendly gesture, born of the kitchen. When your hands were full and your eyes focused on a pan, a simple bump could communicate friendly support. It was never a good idea to pat someone on the bottom uninvited when there were knives close at hand.

But he smiled at her. They all understood his secrets, and his stresses.

Even how critical he had become to the success of the Mbaysey themselves, although he had never wished for something like that.

What would he do in the future when he was finally ready for a new challenge? Something simple, like opening a new bistro in Paris, back on Earth, in the shadow of Gastropode magazine's corporate headquarters?

He laughed at that silly thought, realizing that something like that would be a vacation compared to what he was doing now.

"Let's go shop," he turned his smile to Erin and let her lead.

Tavle Jocia's TradeStation followed most of the standards of deep space. Flat disks several decks thick, each attached to a central housing like lobes on a flower. The station itself was enormous, big enough to include grav field inducers so that everyone could walk around like they were on the surface of a ship, or out on one of the rings on *WinterStar*, where things spun just fast enough to mimic gravity.

The planet below was a blue marble with several connected oceans that produced masses of seafood and such for export. The limited land and relative poverty of heavier elements in the crust meant that industrial products had to be imported from other systems, and the folks who had colonized had brought with them a maritime-style, trade-based culture and economy.

You could find everything on these docks, with a little work and a lot of exercise. Fortunately, Daniel was in far better shape today than a kitchen had ever left him. He could easily keep up with these four women, when he would have been gasping and dragging had he tried to climb this many steps or walk this long a year before.

The docks were at the lowest levels of this lobe, as they were on most, so you climbed stairs to the promenade decks that were in the middle. Personal quarters were above, both for long-term inhabitants as well as the hotels for transients, ranging from simple sleeper coffins all the way up to elaborate suites, such as the one the Trade Factor owned.

Erin brought them out in a place Daniel could only classify as a tourist zone. Everything was pretty and had been painted recently. Pots filled with plants and flowers were everywhere as he looked around, adding a floral undertone to the air and helping clean it.

Even the people he could see, human as well as alien, all seemed to have been touched by the happiness fairy at some point today. He wondered if they were all robots programmed to look cheery at all times.

Worse, they were probably organic, and that behavior had been pounded relentlessly into them.

He looked forward to escaping to one of the grungier

sections of the station, especially given the scent of hot oil he picked up as he followed Erin along. Someplace nearby was cooking lunch by breading it and dropping it into the grease station, probably straight from the freezer and programmed to a specific timer on the package.

He tried to keep the growl of disapproval to himself, but Ndidi had caught it. Or maybe she felt the same way about industrialized food, disseminated from central warehouses off-world aboard those massive transport freighters that carried thousands of shipping containers between worlds.

It made it possible to have a fast food chain that spanned the entirety of the Sept Empire, and had even reached its horrible, gustatory tentacles into the Free Worlds.

Anything to shave a tenth, or even a hundredths of a Crown off costs, in the name of bland mediocrity that could achieve the same low bar of food quality on every planet you ever visited.

"This is all your fault," Iruoma caught up and walked on the side opposite Ndidi.

She had the rudest smile on her face as he turned to her.

"What?" Daniel stammered.

"A year ago, I would have considered that a pleasant meal, worth escaping Ugonna's cooking for," she continued, gesturing with one long arm back at the several nearly-identical storefronts they had finally emerged from. "You have ruined me now forever with your fancy cooking."

Everyone laughed at that.

Ndidi leaned in as they walked and that young woman was positively cruel.

"I'm sure we could talk to Kathra about franchising, Iruoma," she offered with glowing eyes. "Open up a store right there on *WinterStar* so you never have to be without."

"Don't you dare," Iruoma's eyes were bright. "I'd have to

reconsider joining a cloister somewhere. Or something equally pitiful."

"Just making sure," Ndidi laughed. "Wouldn't want you to feel left out or anything."

Daniel smiled with her. Maybe he had made a positive impact on all their lives, after all. Ndidi could certainly handle her own bistro, were he to ever take her back to Genarde with him. The women would never allow someone like Ugonna to cook a pedestrian stew for them again, without an armed revolt.

He felt some of the weight slide off his shoulders.

Maybe he belonged here with these women, after all.

TWELVE

Erin studied the crowd as they walked. She was the tallest person in today's group, although both Kathra and Areen were taller in the inner circle of the comitatus.

Eyes followed them as they walked, but she was used to that. Proud African women, warriors who were taller than most men, stood out. Especially a whole group of them walking together, with a short *Rabic* man in the middle.

Today, she was paying closer attention to the faces turned her way. Who were the ones hunting Daniel? Who reported to Isaev? Who might be spies for the Sept?

Kathra had executed Ugonna for treason, and spread the story, so the Sept knew by now that they had lost their mole. How soon would they try to recruit another? And would it take the form of a woman walking up to join the Mbaysey on this station?

Erin tapped a thumb on her holster as she walked, cognizant that in many ways, the law out here was what you made of it. There was security on the station, but they were mostly concerned, like all stations, with keeping the drunks from causing trouble and making sure that the station inhabitants were safe.

If two outsiders wanted to ruckus with each other, property damage needed to be kept to a minimum. Daniel could affect minds. Erin and her sisters were here in case that wasn't sufficient deterrence.

They had left the friendlier parts of the station, the ones Erin always thought of as a theme park, and moved down into the seedier zones. Where the locals lived and shopped, rather than the travelers and traders. Such places existed on every station, usually down a side corridor where the lighting wasn't as good and maybe the air systems needed to have their filters cleaned a little more regularly than they were.

Cheap places to live. What she was looking for wouldn't be in the bright pavilions out front.

Erin had point today. Joane was right behind her, and Iruoma had the rear, behind Ndidi. The entire situation had left her a little keyed up, but she also hadn't had a good bar fight in a long time, either. Not since before Daniel.

"Let's try here," Ndidi called out as they entered into a wider section of the hallway with stores on each side, like a planet-side shopping mall. There was no mezzanine open above their heads, but the roof had been lifted a little, making this feel more spacious.

Had they lit it adequately, it might have felt quaint instead of despairing.

Erin turned to one side and let Joane and the others pass. She turned back so she could watch the open courtyard in front of her and her team inside. Joane followed the others about halfway and then stationed herself where she could see the rest of the store and Erin at the same time, so her mind was in that same place.

Comitatus.

Warriors.

Killers today, if need be.

She decided to call the open area in front of her a food court. Like it would be out in the pretty spaces, there were several small shops serving food around the walls. Fried. Boiled. Dried. No smell bad enough to turn her stomach, but obviously the sort of place where you ate when your cash flow was having problems, but you still needed protein and calories.

Not quite Skid Row, to use the old human term, but you could probably see it from here. Maybe even get there if you weren't careful. Erin imagined that the station would handle vagrancy by putting your lazy ass on a shuttle to the surface. Or maybe selling you to a ship needing crew as a way to pay off fines.

The Free Worlds might be free, but they were also a little rough.

It didn't help her state of mind that about half the people she could see weren't human. And not just normal aliens you saw on many stations, like the Se'uh'pal that reminded her of walking rabbits, or the Vida snake people that slithered on a lower half.

If she remembered correctly, the thing directly across the way was an Atter. Certainly, it had the three legs and three arms. Three eyes and three mouths. Green and taller than her, they had reminded Erin of a walking cactus. Didn't move much faster, either.

And there was no way to tell if it was watching her, since there was always one eye in her direction, regardless of which way the legs carried the creature. Erin shrugged internally and mostly ignored the creature. Any of them could outrun it, and she couldn't see an obvious weapon on the harness circling that columnar body. Might be hidden under the three-way skirt, but she'd just deal with it if that became a problem.

Erin glanced back and caught Joane's nod. No trouble so far. She turned her head back to the big space and scowled her disdain at anyone and everyone, just to see who might take offense.

Kathra was a master of that maneuver. She could attack an entire hall with it and immediately locate the three people who held ill will, just by the way they blinked.

If you didn't care, you didn't notice. If you had a problem with Kathra Omezi, your hackles would come up like a cat's, even before you realized it.

Nobody rose angrily from one of the long tables out in front of her, indignant for reasons they might not even recognize. That was good. Erin was feeling maybe a touch feisty today, and really didn't care if she had to hurt someone in the process. Might possibly be looking forward to it, although she would never suggest that out loud.

She did get somebody's attention. Looked like a somebody.

Blue. Weird.

Pale blue hair. Darker blue skin. Like maybe one of those blond NorthEuros after you dipped them in blue wood stain for a bit and then let it run off.

Looking this way, and then down in what Erin might have classified as embarrassment when they locked eyes.

Close to human, from what Erin could see. Basic outline was there. Same for the face, although it was hard to tell from this far across the way. Something was off, but blue already told her the person she was staring at wasn't human.

Female, maybe. Had the right shape, curvier rather than blocky. Was eating her lunch or something over there, just minding her own business, except for the way her eyes came up and stared every few seconds.

Erin paid attention to the rest of the space, on the off-chance she was dealing with some sort of honey-trap situation, but nobody else was even looking. She turned to Joane and nodded the woman closer. Might be worth rattling someone's tree, just to see what fell out.

Kathra had warned Erin and the others that they might have to play a little rough.

Might be time to see.

THIRTEEN

It was still weird, being considered enough a member of the comitatus to join them in the field. Ndidi wasn't armed, not like the other three, but she had a nice boning knife tucked into a pocket she had sewn to her thigh, where they had holsters.

Still, she was the least dangerous person here, and she knew it. Wasn't even offended by it, because Kathra herself had explained the need for Ndidi's brains in situations where the others might immediately resort to brawn.

Daniel was shopping. She had heard the story told enough times to understand that he didn't know what he was looking for, except that it would be exotic and alien. Like a book written in K'bari, punched and put into a ring-binger that had originally been a Sept kitchen manual.

There was an even better story there than the contents themselves, but they would never hear it. That was a shame, because someone had found the book and salvaged it. How many other things like that just went out the trashlock to burn up in an atmosphere, rather than being saved for a future need.

Iruoma was standing close to Daniel as they looked at old books. Things that might be written in a language nobody could even recognize, let alone understand.

How many written languages were there among the stars? Even Earth and the Sept Empire had dozens that had come into space over the last two thousand years.

Other cultures, she had read, generally settled into something of a monoculture before making the leap outward to galactic civilization, but humans had been contacted early or something. Given the ability to escape the home system while there were still enough different cultures that human might yet come to be a byword for chaos with some of the better regimented species.

Or not. Who knew what space travel did to well-laid plans?

Ndidi was over in the hardware section of what could passably be called a junk store. Clothing filled a large chunk of the front, because finding things that fit in a store was rare, which was why the Mbaysey just bought cloth and made their own, most of the time. Or like Daniel, brought money with them and then could shop in stores like this and find things that fit.

These three aisles were hard to describe. Good, working electronics were in a glass case close to the proprietor, where you might ask to inspect something under his watchful eye. Things that could be easily dismantled and repurposed were over a row.

This was the leftovers.

Ndidi wasn't a technician. She'd leave that sort of thing to Joane, who had an eye for it.

Today she was just touching things and judging them. Simple bits could be cut and welded from sheet and bar stock that *ForgeStar* produced. Other things could be printed using base materials that several of the clans specialized in.

This was junk nobody wanted anymore.

It had had value once. Someone had needed it, found it, bought it, carried it into space.

But it had ended up here.

A small pink cube small enough to fit in her palm seemed to stand out from all the black or gray cases around it, so Ndidi reached out a hand and grasped it.

Cool. Heavy in her hand, as though mostly metal, rather than some polymer.

The faces were all featureless, save for a button on one side, so she pressed it.

The cube leapt out of her hands before she could grasp it, and then hovered in the air rather than falling to the deck. It seemed to be glowing, but she couldn't see what else it might be doing.

Ndidi shrugged and had reached out a hand to grab it again, when she saw points of light on her hand. It was a projector of some sort.

She put both hands close around it and saw lights like pinpricks showing on her hand. It didn't want to move when she touched it, so Ndidi pressed the power button and suddenly it was just a heavy cube again, which she nearly dropped before she got fingers all the way around it.

Voices broke her out of her reverie. Daniel and Iruoma stepped close.

"Something's up," he said. "Find something?"

Ndidi looked around and realized that Joane had moved to the door and was standing close to Erin, deep in some quiet conversation that involved looking both directions like hawks.

"Maybe," she turned her attention back to Daniel and held it up.

He studied it for a moment, but shrugged without comment. She had spent enough time around the man to know he had just asked all the voices in his head if anyone recognized it, and nobody had.

It must be a weird way to live, but it gave him an entire encyclopedia to call on, which made up for it.

Ndidi turned and walked purposefully to the proprietor, a fat human with skin like dark butter. He studied her for a second, and then the others.

"Two Guilders," he muttered.

Ndidi didn't have all day, since Erin needed backup, but she wasn't about to just pay the asking price.

In the end, she got him down to one sloth and two fifths. And only took a minute to get there.

Ndidi slid the cube into a pouch on her left thigh and followed the others to whatever trouble seemed to be brewing out front.

FOURTEEN

ONCE THE OTHERS JOINED HER, Erin stepped out of the store and looked for an excuse to cause a little trouble. The blue girl was still there, delicately eating a soup or something. It involved a spoon, whatever she was doing.

"Problems?" Iruoma asked as she stepped close.

"Unlikely, but I'm going to push," Erin replied in a low voice.

She moved, confident that the others would follow. The meeting later was one that Daniel needed to attend, now that the rich man had had a chance to send his people over and look at the ship. Kathra would come over to the station later with a second group, but Erin had wanted an afternoon to scout the station for trouble.

Even if she had to make some up.

She moved to a place serving human food. Udon noodles in broth with choice of protein from the menu over the counter.

"Small standard with shrimp," she said as the tiny *Spanic* man behind the counter looked up at her.

She watched him ladle everything into a cheap bowl and

add broth, uncaring if it was any good. It was possible to screw up something so basic, but for one Guilder, she wouldn't be out anything she minded, if she ended up taking one sip and trashing it.

Daniel was right behind her as she paid and ordered the same, only with chicken, but the others remained out on the concourse watching everything.

She hadn't mentioned the girl, so nobody else was locked on her right now. That was good. The blue girl ate slowly and looked this direction occasionally, just as she had earlier when Erin was across the way.

Watching.

Daniel paid as she walked out and stood with the others. He joined her a moment later and she set off across the way, bowl and spoon in hand.

The middle of the food court area was largely empty. Mid-afternoon by local clocks, more or less, so halfway between lunch and dinner crowds, if such a thing happened around here.

Erin walked to the table directly in front of the blue girl and sat down with her back to the woman. She nodded Daniel into the space directly across from her, more or less staring at the girl from about four meters away, and the others took up spots around them.

She tasted the udon enough to know that it wasn't bad. Rich with flavor, even. Thick noodles. Size sixty shrimp inside. Hot enough to scald her mouth right now, so she just sipped a little and blew on it.

Erin caught Daniel's eye wand nodded. He was also sipping the udon, but appeared to be enjoying himself, so maybe this was what it was supposed to taste like. She'd never eaten Nihonese food growing up. Simple vegetables in broth had been her limit, occasionally with meat, frequently with noodles. Kathra's mother, Yagazie, had been too poor to really do much, other than make sure everyone had nutritious food.

It had taken her daughter years to build up the relative wealth to hire an outsider who could teach them about good food.

"Behind me," she said simply, focusing her eyes on his.

"Blue?" he murmured back.

Erin nodded.

He glanced that way a little longer, like a *male* might do with a pretty woman in a public place. They were like that when there wasn't a woman to keep them in line.

Daniel turned back to her and nodded with only his eyes,

"Threat?" she asked.

His eyes got a little big and then he put down his bowl of noodles and his chopsticks.

A big breath swelled that scrawny chest for a moment, and then his eyes started to glow, ever so slightly.

You had to know what to look for in order to see it, but Daniel Lémieux had just stepped outside of himself.

FIFTEEN

He hated to do this. At the same time, he understood the need.

Daniel looked at the stranger one last time and then took hold of her mind as delicately as he could. Doing this with Mikhail Isaev he'd been a little more gruff. Maybe left the man with a headache on purpose afterwards, just for making him sit inside the mind of a sociopath with almost no human empathy whatsoever.

Probably made Isaev a better businessman, since he generally didn't care who he hurt, but for Daniel, it would have probably just been less painful to have Kathra or someone punch him in the face with a fist for an hour.

Hopefully, the woman was different.

Blueness, distilled down into a mostly human form.

Cobalt hair. Periwinkle skin. Navy eyes with starkly bright whites around them.

Head more triangular than a human, seen face-on. Prominent forehead and larger eyes tapering down past dominating cheekbones to a tiny jaw.

Horizontal eyeslits, rather than the vertical which seemed more common, from what he had seen of other aliens.

Female. Close enough to the standard bipedal form that she could pass as human woman with a little work and low lighting.

Daniel reached out carefully, cognizant that someone on this station had touched him before and then vanished.

Her emotions were loud as he listened, rather than shielded away behind some barrier that might hide her.

Nervous. Skittish at the group of dark-skinned strangers that had moved so close, but not quite ready to flee. Tempted to talk to them, maybe. They were so close.

Daniel ground his teeth together and swallowed the sudden ball of rage that had formed in his mouth that he had to do this.

He touched her mind.

It was like opening a randomly-pulled book down from the shelf and letting it fall open on the table.

She was alone. Afraid. Lost.

He pushed a little, moving past the surface of her mind like a diver entering the water.

Species: Kaniea. A form that had evolved similar to human from similar environments and the way physics affected everyone. Blue to his pinkish brown. Three slender fingers and a long thumb on each hand instead of four.

Close enough for government work.

Why are you here?

He didn't form the words directly into her mind so much as trigger them to see what memories responded. Urid-Varg had taught his victims many useful things you could do inside someone else's mind.

Daniel felt like the worst of any two evils right now, but it was necessary. A stranger had gotten Erin's attention in a bad way.

He watched images of the woman.

Girl. She wasn't much older than Ndidi, who was herself young enough to be his own daughter.

Warrior, too. Proud child on what Daniel's brain kept wanting to interpret as a coming-of-age quest. Except she'd never returned to her homeworld, drawn to seek something greater than a mere sign from the gods.

Or maybe the gods had bigger plans for her.

She had a name, too, once he dug deep enough.

A'Alhakoth ver'Shingi. It conveyed rank and importance within her culture. Not quite a princess, but not a peasant either.

Just a young woman far from home.

Daniel saw no threat, so he reached across the table and took Erin's hand. Shared his mind with her, that she could turn around inside herself and see this stranger, this warrior youth named A'Alhakoth.

In Kathra's service, he could convince himself that it wasn't rape, to open a woman's innermost thoughts like this and study them. Felt like it, though. He'd want a long shower when this day was done, but he did not do it for himself.

As long as Daniel kept telling himself that, he wasn't evil.

Erin's mind turned back to his after a few seconds of study.

"New recruit?" she asked.

"Kathra's call, but I see nothing disqualifying her," Daniel replied.

"I meant comitatus," Erin clarified.

"I know," he said. "And Kathra would have me do the same thing to her then, instead of taking the initiative to do it now."

"Understood."

Erin separated herself and he let go.

A'Alhakoth must have sensed something had occurred,

because suddenly her heart was racing. She was on the verge of bolting, when what she really needed was a friend.

It wouldn't be him. Especially not once she found out what he could do. No woman would ever trust him once they learned that truth.

But he reached out and quietly took hold of her emotions with an iron fist. Carefully, he wound everything back down until she was calm.

He let go finally and looked down into his broth.

So little time had passed that a sip was still almost too hot handle, but hopefully it would do something about the pounding in his head.

He watched Erin stand up, turn around, and seat herself across from the other woman.

SIXTEEN

Erin watched the girl like she would a new recruit auditioning for a spot in the comitatus. All of those women met her standards before they ever got presented to Kathra.

Daniel had done something to the woman. Erin could tell that just from the way her breath had slowed all the way back down to normal over the last five seconds. And from having been inside her mind just a little before that.

She knew Daniel was feeling like a shit right now, for having done it, but he had followed her orders. Erin had been inside his head enough to know that it would help his state of mind that way. He didn't think it was as evil when someone else ordered him to use his powers.

"Kaniea?" Erin asked politely. As if she didn't already know the girl's species.

The girl nodded, navy blue eyes hooded under brows that weren't all that heavy, but conveyed seriousness of intent right now. And she spoke common Spacer well enough to follow the conversation.

"We're human," Erin continued. "Tribal affiliation Mbaysey. I'm Erin Uduik."

Another nod. Not offering a name back, but that was fine. Strangers. Strange place.

Anybody spending any time in the Free Worlds would have picked up some level of Spacer, regardless of what they spoke at home. Erin just had to pretend that the girl might not be as fluent as Erin knew she really was.

Erin watched the woman. Behind her, the others were paying attention, but nobody had moved to do anything. They would also be watching their corners for others coming along with an unwelcome attention to the group from *WinterStar*.

The blue woman watched her now. Processing, from the way her eyes flickered over Erin's shoulders to take in the others.

Erin could have told her that A'Alhakoth ver'Shingi had no meaningful secrets, but then she would have to explain how she knew that.

Nobody was ready for that conversation, just yet, but Erin also knew she could trust this woman's world and character. That was a powerful tool, to be able to recruit someone and *know* who they were.

Even if it made Daniel a little evil. She'd make it up to the man later somehow.

"Is there a reason you chose to join me?" A'Alhakoth ver'Shingi asked in a cool, modulated voice almost as deep as Erin's alto.

One hand wanted to stray off the table, but she kept it in sight. Erin didn't even move, sure that the folks behind her could react faster than the blue woman could.

"You looked like someone alone and far from home," Erin replied honestly.

She did, and it was a very brutal truth.

If you wanted to travel the galaxy, you either had to be extremely wealthy, or work odd jobs along the way.

A'Alhakoth was getting down to the point where she'd have to find a job soon.

"So?" the blue woman asked bluntly.

"So we're about to set off on a grand adventure towards the center of the galaxy, from the distant rims where we've been," Erin said. "The Commander put me in charge of recruiting around here, looking for folks that might have a better feel for those sectors."

As lies went, this one was pretty believable, and Kathra would back her up one hundred percent if asked. Second in command of the comitatus meant Erin had a tremendous leeway for interpreting things, as long as she understood that enough mistakes in judgement on her part might force her to give way to someone like Areen or Iruoma.

Not that much would change if that happened.

The woman studied her for a long second. Erin could see that *too-good-to-be-true* gleam in her eyes. Understood it.

A gift horse walking up and offering three wishes, to mix all the metaphors wrong.

"You know the kaniea?" A'Alhakoth asked, surprised if Erin was reading the tone of her voice correctly.

That girl was a long ways from home.

"I do not," Erin said. "Daniel recognized your kind and gave me some of the details."

"Daniel?"

Erin turned and looked over her shoulder.

"Daniel, Ndidi, could you join us?" she said conversationally.

Joane and Iruoma would go back to being paranoid hawks watching her flanks now, with Erin and Ndidi facing the other way.

The blue woman studied the three of them with a nervous twitch that hadn't been there a moment ago. Possibly feeling a little outnumbered, but Erin didn't offer to send Ndidi over to balance things out a little.

Let you face up to three on one odds and show us what you're made of.

"I'm Daniel," he said simply. "I've researched the kaniea, as well as the anndaing, the ch'sh'xx, and the K'bari. We'll actually be looking for some K'bari worlds, and I think they lie in the same general direction as your homeworlds, not quite as far in and a little driftward."

"K'bari?"

She seemed astounded. Like maybe they were legends from her people, one of the lost tribes that had more or less faded out. Many species did that after a while, although Erin didn't think humans would ever fall into that category.

Daniel said something in a language Erin had never heard. The girl nearly levitated out of her seat when he did, so it must have been good.

Or one of the ghosts in the man's head spoke kaniea well enough.

Her eyeslits opened all the way up when she got nervous like this, that much was obvious.

Erin wondered if she had read the girl right. Maybe had pushed her a little too hard, from the way the eyes got even bigger.

She seemed set to bolt.

"We're in wing four, bay seventeen," Erin said to her, trying to cut through the noise.

It was obvious that Daniel was just letting her deal with things now, rather than doing anything to calm the woman.

"What are you people?" A'Alhakoth asked.

"Humans," Daniel said quietly. "Seekers, looking for something we think is hidden deeper into the central areas."

He turned to look at Erin now, a question in his eyes. She nodded permission.

"We are looking for ways to flee the Free Worlds and the Sept entirely and irrevocably," he continued, his voice growing lower and turning into more of a growl. "To build a better life for the tribe someplace where the people here can't chase us. As Erin said, we're looking for scouts we can hire."

Erin figured that they'd done enough damage to this poor, periwinkle woman. She rose abruptly and stepped back, pausing to grab her bowl and slip the travel lid back over it so she didn't spill any.

"Safe travels," she said as Daniel and Ndidi rose a beat later, a little confused but not saying anything. "Four seventeen if you change your mind."

She turned and walked away, confident that the others would watch anything behind her. A'Alhakoth needed time to decide if she really wanted to walk off a cliff and try to find a place on an alien starship, but anybody would. Erin only knew what she was capable of, not what she would actually do.

Kinda like the rest of them.

SEVENTEEN

SHE ALREADY KNEW that the man seated across from her was something of a sleazeball, but he was also her best choice for what she needed next, so Kathra had put up with the sly innuendos and subtle invitations she had no interest in pursuing.

Based on what Daniel had said, the man was just wired that way, and probably didn't even recognize it himself. To Factor Isaev, every woman was a potential prize to be pursued and conquered, for no other reason than the conquest itself.

It didn't seem to matter to him that she was slightly taller, much stronger, and utterly repulsed at the thought of his touch. If anything, that probably heightened the desire on Isaev's part.

So she had dressed for war her way tonight. Erin and the others had worn what generally worked as the uniform of the comitatus when they had to be on a station for a reasonable period of time.

Heavy boots to mid-calf designed for planetside terrain as well as station treads. They were a rough, matte brown that didn't require stupid amounts of time and effort to keep clean, mostly because Kathra didn't believe in lining all the women up for inspection.

If you were in the comitatus, you were good. If you started to slack, the others snapped you back into place, or Kathra would eventually retire you out to flying SkyCamels. Same with new mothers. You stopped flying combat missions when you had a daughter waiting at home for you.

The comitatus these days was wearing long pants tucked in and made from a reasonably heavy denim they had found at Soomi, someone closing out nearly one hundred long-bolts of the stuff, all in a soft orange somewhere midway between sand and flame. Daniel had called the color tangerine, and that name had stuck.

Jackets were the same material, lined and then waterproofed, because every damned TradeStation has thermostats controlled by men and kept three to five degrees cooler than Kathra kept *WinterStar*. Black pullover shirts under the jackets stood out against the brightness of the fabric.

Like the rest of her women, Kathra had a pistol strapped to her thigh, available in a hurry if she needed to take someone down with a compact particle projector fed by ammunition disks. Splatter someone's silly ass all over the place.

The only thing that really marked Kathra different from her women was the half-cloak she had added tonight. It hooked loosely at the neck, but not so tight that someone could grab it and control her. Like the uniform, it was tangerine, but edged in two embroidered colors, black at the outside and blue a finger inside that.

Standing with the rest of the women out in the salon, it made her look like a Commander, rather than a poor, tribal leader seeking favor.

Kathra Omezi granted favors to lesser beings.

If you were lucky.

Trade Factor Isaev turned to her now, as his majordomo finished delivering coffee and tea to everyone and seated himself. That put four on the far side of the table, with two new people, both male, who looked more like mechanics than anything. Possibly retired ones that had gone into yacht design, or something similar.

She had Daniel, Erin, and Ndidi, while half a dozen others waited outside in the salon, presumably making Isaev's employees nervous. The men he had on staff were obviously guards, some of them even looking professional enough, while the women were all domestics.

Pretty ones, too, doe-eyes and rather stupid looking, so Kathra had no doubt that they served double duty in this household.

She fixed her eyes on Isaev and dared him to spend the next hour on blandishments and irrelevancies, like a Sept gentleman greeting a distant relative of unknown provenance.

He seemed to understand her game, not that she was trying all that hard to conceal it. And while he was the biggest game in town, he wasn't the only one. Plus, this wasn't the only system in the Free Worlds capable of building warships for her.

"So we have studied the specifications of the four ships you currently have on offer," the Factor began abruptly, surprising only the people on his side of the table. "My experts tell me that none of that technology is all that common in human space, and some of it completely unknown."

"So my people tell me," Daniel spoke up serenely.

Kathra scowled so she didn't grin at the understanding of who *Daniel's people* were.

"All of them are in flyable condition right now, but none

come equipped with a valence drive, so they are shuttles functionally, rather than interstellar yachts," the Factor continued.

"Yes," Kathra agreed blandly. "I brought them here aboard *WinterStar* when I transported Daniel."

"The price you are asking for them is impossible," Isaev said.

He really didn't mean it. That much was obvious from the gleam in his eyes. They were just down to the dickering stage. Earlier than she had expected, even.

"For four shuttle craft each not much larger than two SkyCamels put together, I would agree," Kathra smiled at the man, turning to include his three flunkies in the look. "However, you have nothing like them in your collection, nor does anyone else. Plus, you can incorporate the technology included in them with new vessels your yards put out, so you will be able to charge exotic, new prices and have a psychological leg up on your competition, for however long it takes one of them to steal the ideas themselves."

"And you will not tell us where you even found them?" Isaev asked.

"Correct," Kathra smiled and leaned back. "Part of the reason I wish to commission a ship from you, or purchase one and have it modified, is so we can go look in places where Daniel's predecessors traveled, to see what other interesting things we might find."

"Ram cannons are illegal on civilian vessels," the Factor pointed out.

"The Mbaysey are a stellar nation unto themselves, Trade Factor," Kathra let her tone get sharp and deadly now. "This vessel will become part of my navy. Plus, we will not be spending any significant time in the Free Worlds, other than to cross to a border and exit. Similarly, we will return at some point, and I'd prefer if any pirates out there decided there was easier game to be had."

"How many other vessels do you foresee selling in the future?" Isaev asked, splitting his glance between her and Daniel now.

Daniel shrugged. Kathra smiled.

"Not all of them are even flyable, at present, and some may never be repairable, either," she said. "A few are so alien that it will take us time to translate the old manuals and notes, before we could, in good conscience, sell them to someone else."

She liked the way his eyes flickered at that. Just a moment of greed so deep it was like that cartoon duck swimming in a lake of gold coins.

Alien tech might be better than human. Someone capable of understanding such tech and building new ships might have such a head start on their competitors that it took a generation to catch up. What amount of money was that worth?

Yes, she knew where this man's pressure points were, courtesy of Daniel. And she began to understand the nature of evil as he saw it.

If no one could stop you, the urge to just take something from someone might be overwhelming after a while. You could change the world, make it a better place, but only so far as you saw it. Others might disagree.

Changing them to see things your way was an evil comparable to six strong men pinning a woman down and taking turns at her.

So she had instructed Daniel to just observe tonight, leaving his native paranoia against unwelcome surprises, but not reading or affecting the Trade Factor while they worked.

Kathra had no idea if the man might come to understand what had happened later, or work through his own mind when she was gone and perhaps find the welds and seams from someone working on his psyche. Best not to leave any.

After all, if this worked, she might bring back several more vessels to auction off. Wouldn't do to have alienated the wealthiest man in the sector at that point.

Even if she didn't end up selling some of the stranger vessels. After all, not every species had used a valence drive as humans understood it, even if physics was physics.

"So it is in my interest in making you a deal for a good vessel," the Trade Factor laughed after a moment. "That you can make it back safe, as well as feel some level of obligation for such a deal?"

Kathra smiled about a millimeter deep at the man. In essence, he was correct.

"Some of the legends I am pursuing involve something other than a valence drive to travel between worlds," Daniel spoke up now.

The effect was similar to a large asteroid slamming into a small planet. All four of the men on the other side cried out in shock or negation, but fell silent a moment later when they realized that she and Daniel were serious.

"Surely, that is impossible, Commander," Isaev ventured.

"Surely," she agreed with a serene smile. "But what would a vessel be worth to a naval shipyard, if they could use something different. Possibly better?"

It was like the Goddess of Avarice had come down from the Sky Hells and seated herself at the end of the table, just touching each of those men with her stellar staff in turn. Faces flushed, which was exceptionally obvious when all four were *Anglos*. Breathing got heavy and rushed. Eyes went wide and lost focus on the present tense.

"Good, you understand me finally," Kathra said.

"Warships require a denser crew than civilian ships, even carriers," one of the mechanics finally spoke up.

The taller of the two. Younger by a few years, but not anybody that Kathra found interesting enough to remember. If nothing else, he was *male*. Daniel was enough male for her command vessel, and he had earned his place. Let these pitiful creatures go back to their natural place in the nursery or the classroom.

Or learn to cook.

"I have begun accepting resumes," Kathra said, laughing inside as she had exactly one so far, and that because of Erin. "Understand that preference of place will go to women already in the Mbaysey, aboard one of the ClanStars, but if there are a few worthy men here, they might find spaces with the Clans, replacing those women."

The rudeness of that statement, in this group, was worth it alone. The Free Worlds were more open-minded about many things than the Sept Empire, not that they were all that much better at the end of the day. Tavle Jocia, at least this TradeStation, was still dominated and largely owned by males.

She could have taken her business to places where the women were mostly in charge, like Cylou, but they were too close to the Sept Border for Kathra to feel comfortable. A Septagon or a few Patrols could slip quietly across the border and be upon her before she could do anything but run, possibly costing her dearly if she had teams on the station who couldn't escape in the mess.

Maybe she needed to modify a few SkyCamels with valence drives, just in case. It would play hell with their cargo capacity, but one vessel in six would allow all the pilots to escape if that happened.

Kathra made a note to inquire with her flight deck leaders.

"Would any other men be welcome to fly with you, if

some volunteered?" Isaev asked, trying to find a loophole he could exploit.

Certainly, the man didn't have a high enough opinion of women to send a spy into their midst that way.

"Men are always welcome to apply," Kathra said, still smiling. "We maintain a population of around fifteen percent, once vetted, to meet most of our procreative needs. They work on one of the ClanStars as artists or farm hands. A few eventually find their way to *ForgeStar* or *IronStar*, doing heavier labor and metal-bashing. All the crew of *WinterStar* are female except Daniel. All the crew of this new vessel will be as well."

"Have you considered an armored cruiser, instead?" the other mechanic asked. "If you built a larger vessel, you could include standard grav field inducers and follow a different architecture. Sturdier and more resilient."

"We're comfortable with a ship that spins along a central axis and has a thick ring hanging from the center for the flight deck and the living quarters," Kathra said. "*WinterStar* is starting to show his age, and we would rather have a purpose-built warship that could carry a larger comitatus, say perhaps sixty or eighty Spectres instead of twenty-five. Plus Ram Cannons in case we need to pummel something into submission. We will still fight at carrier distances. Plus, grav field inducers are large and wasteful of mass and energy. I have no interest in building something as large as a Septagon at present. It is enough to drive off a Sept Patrol with their noses thoroughly bloodied."

Kathra liked the way the two mechanics clammed up, and the majordomo's mouth fell open when she suggested building a Septagon. Let them know she was thinking large in the future. And dangerous.

Worse, that she might be able to afford something like

that, with whatever treasure she brought back from the unknown depths of space.

Isaev smiled finally, greed welling up and snuffing out all his good sense. Like, why would Kathra Omezi want her own Septagon? What would she do with something like that?

She had no idea. The Star Turtle already had enough space that she could move the entire Mbaysey over there if she chose, and live comfortably.

But a new ship, a big one, would let her find a new series of stars to call a homeland. Not that she would ever colonize the surface of a planet again, but if she was far enough away from everybody else, then her grandchildren might decide to.

She would live out her time in space, where no Septagon could catch her.

EIGHTEEN

Pasdar strode out onto the Great Causeway of Septagon Vorgash's Command Node. Aspbad Rostami was already present, midway through his own command shift as final adjustments and last minute hiccups were addressed.

With an undertaking this grand, there were always bound to be glitches. A good commander did not demand perfection. He demanded answers and implementation plans. Rostami had a good crew under him.

"Are we ready?" Pasdar asked the man as he came to rest.

Ahead of him, out the windows, the tip of the Septagon seemed to point like a bowsprit into deep space. Not entirely the unknown, but certainly a place none of them had ever been before.

"We are, Naupati," Rostami replied with pride in his voice. "Forward Operating Base Urmia has signaled their readiness."

"Open a channel to the entire squadron," Pasdar ordered.

None of his other ships were visible from here. The two Patrols Vorgash carried were docked for transit, and the others were ranging ahead, but most of the resupply ships were within range of his voice right now.

After all, it wasn't every day that the Sept Empire invaded the Free Worlds.

And even this wasn't technically an invasion. Pasdar had no intention of attacking any of the Free Worlds themselves, or to engage with whatever defensive forces they might field, other than to drive them off if they chose to protect Kathra Omezi and her so-called Mbaysey Tribal Squadron.

If so, then he would simply crush them before moving on. Scorched earth worked just fine, after all, when your target cannot feed themselves otherwise.

Rostami nodded to him and stepped back into a parade rest position.

"Vorgash Operating Squadron, this is Naupati Amirin Pasdar," he said in a voice perhaps ranging over into pride, at least more than was his normal wont. The Lords of the Sept Fleet had chosen him after all, and his crews to do this thing.

"We are about to set out on a punitive expedition today," he continued. "We will cross the Free Worlds, but not engage them. It is even possible we will trade with some systems. In others, you will build forward operating bases such as Urmia behind us. Septagon Vorgash will lead into the darkness, seeking our foe, but we can sail no farther, no faster than the work of all of the support vessels allows. Keep that in mind when you approach your jobs, because every box you deliver is as important as any Ram Cannon gunner firing a shot into our foe. More important, because those gunners can only get there to deliver the killing shot because you have done the hard work necessary ahead of time."

Pasdar paused to take a breath and let himself pace. It aided his thought processes. These words would be recorded and played back later, either in his victory parade or his disgrace.

"In the whole of the Sept Empire, Vorgash was chosen for this mission. You men were chosen for this mission."

Pasdar skipped over the women aboard the mighty vessel. As sex servants, they served no useful purpose in the fighting, merely assisting with crew morale by being available for physical release.

"We are about to exit the Sept Empire itself," Pasdar continued. "We will seek our destiny in the darkness of the Free Worlds, but even that will only be temporary, as our foe will seek to hide in the spaces beyond. We will chase them there as well, running them down like a cat taking down an eland, until they lay supine at our feet."

His pacing had taken him all the way to the front of the Command Node, so he turned back to look at the men behind him, and the squadron that he would lead into unknown regions, however metaphorically.

"I expect each of you to work hard and pay attention, that we may complete our mission as soon as possible and return home covered in glory by the Emperor and his servants. That is the thing they have laid on our shoulders, my comrades. The Glory of the Emperor himself. Now, all vessels stand by for transition to valence drives."

Pasdar let his pacing take him to where Rostami was standing above one of his officers, watching a read-out on a screen. He looked up now and nodded.

Pasdar smiled and considered his destiny, laid out in front of him.

"All vessels depart."

NINETEEN

Daniel sighed and scowled at the man once more. They were down in the bowels of the alien transport, alone and cramped, with some of the engine machinery open and a toolbox that left almost no space for movement.

Or for a sense of humor.

It wasn't that the mechanic was stupid, so much as utterly hidebound in his ways. That made him quite possibly the most wrong person for this job that Daniel could think of, but they were not his Guilders being spent, except as measured by the time he had to spend training this numbskull to do this job.

"It's not metric, just like it is not imperial," Daniel explained, again. "That's why the sockets and screws are lettered rather than numbered. If you ask for a G-socket, it's going to be different from a number seven. We can't even use a multi-pin shifter, unless you rebuild one on seven-tenths of a millimeter scale instead of the standard one millimeter you have in your tool box."

"Then why not pull it all out and replace it with

metrics?" the man asked stupidly, for something like the third time.

"What you do tomorrow is not my problem," Daniel finally snapped at the man. "If you manage to break it after the sale is complete, then Isaev can pay you or someone else to repair it. But I will have trained you correctly, *connard*."

"Why did they do it differently?" the moron asked, like a stupid bulldog on a particularly tasty bone.

"They didn't," Daniel said. "We did. This ship was built by a species with four arms ending in tentacles, rather than fingers. Their understanding of how to lathe bolts followed the same physics, but a different starting point. A G-socket is not a number seven. It is actually about a six and a quarter, if you wanted to strip irreplaceable bolts in your comical ineptness."

"Hey," the man finally barked, having gotten almost as angry as Daniel.

That, in turn, caused him to surge upright and smash his forehead into a pipe with a thunk that almost sounded like the moron had managed to crack bone. Pretty impressive, considering how thick his skull had become to new ideas.

"Are you finally paying attention?" Daniel growled.

"Problems in there?" Joane's voice suddenly wafted into the crawlspace from where she and several others of the comitatus were keeping watch.

"Shut up and do it my way, or you'll break the damned thing," Daniel hissed quietly at the man. "Are you listening?"

He wasn't. Not really. But if Daniel could say that the fool knew how to open the engines and read the manual on how to service them, then a huge chunk of credit would pass from the accounts of Mikhail Isaev into those of Kathra Omezi, on their way right back into Isaev's hands once he finished building her a warship.

If you didn't need grav field inducers installed and

painstakingly calibrated, the rest was physics and programming a fabrication robot to turn out the same section of hull enough times to build a ring five times wider than *WinterStar*'s.

The worker pulled his hand down from his forehead and looked at it.

"You aren't bleeding," Daniel told him. "Grow up and act like a professional."

The man wanted to say something, but even Daniel felt the rage in his eyes and hands right now. It might be like a rabid chipmunk attacking a dog, but the dog would know he'd been bled before he won.

And he might not win.

"Fine," the man said. "Hand me the H-socket, the extender, and shift the light to your right about thirty degrees so I can see."

Daniel did. It would take time for the man to learn everything. Daniel had been forced to translate memories as well as ancient records, and then have *IronStar* turn him out an entirely new, custom tool set capable of handling all the maintenance tasks. Plans for that set, in addition to the one version done in steel, were part of the reason Isaev had been willing to make a deal.

Each of the four custom ships came with bespoke tool sets and measurements to turn out more. And each one of them was slightly different, even with something as basic as a machine-threaded bolt.

But Isaev would have something nobody else in this part of the galaxy had. And he would lord it over the other men who had made a name for themselves as gearheads, just as he would most likely strip these four ships down to the bulkheads so he could study them.

Isaev Heavy Foundries was probably about ten years from upsetting the natural order of things in this sector, if they could fully exploit the tech Kathra had decided to make available.

Daniel was looking forward to finding something really powerful out there. Something that could change the balance of power between the Free Worlds and the Sept. With the Sept and all their neighbors, who had to fear that hand reaching out for them next. A new stardrive they could sell after installing. Better weapon systems than a Ram Cannon or Heavy Particle Cannon that was the current state of the art. Something that would give the Commander a decisive edge over the Sept itself.

The Turtle was alien, but there was no technology there that he could disseminate, other than the various shuttles, none of which were armed.

The mechanic shut his mouth finally and backed out a set of bolts as Daniel watched in silence. Behind that were the louvres and other controls for the fuel feeds. This vessel cracked water for hydrogen, ionized it to break the bonds, and then did something with fusion and a few other things beyond Daniel's experience to generate thrust. Not a particular improvement over other systems in use, but a completely new way of doing things, and perhaps somebody would come up with something even better by studying it.

As long as Isaev claimed all the credit for the innovations, nobody would come looking for Daniel Lémieux and ask how he had come to know these things. Because he already knew that there were people out there, looking for him. The Sept would not forget Kathra Omezi. Someone had touched him once and withdrawn, but he still didn't think he had imagined it.

It felt like they were just biding their time until they could attack.

TWENTY

The four ships were sold. Financial magic had happened. The future suddenly looked almost bright.

Erin had decided to celebrate on the station with a few of the girls. And make herself visible.

Kathra had been serious about expanding the tribe, but only following the old rules. Small groups of friends were preferable to singles or mobs. New recruits went to work farming on a ClanStar until they proved themselves otherwise, except for very specific technical specialists.

And Erin didn't think they would find another rock-star chef out of work. Not clear out here. But Daniel and Ndidi had trained up replacements who were already better than Ugonna on her best day, and getting better with every meal.

So Erin was on the station for a night of drinking and maybe a little fighting, just to prove to herself that she still had it. Baby-making wasn't anywhere on her schedule yet, although she knew Kathra would come after her at some point.

Probably so that their daughters could be born together and grow up as cousins.

The SkyCamel docked at the usual airlock. Station Control had pretty much just assigned it to them at this point, since they had been coming and going so frequently. And it helped that the Trade Factor who owned most of the people on the station could pull strings.

"You girls ready?" Erin asked as she powered everything down and unbuckled.

Iruoma growled happily. Stina and Kam were at the rear hatch, all set to go, looking almost like day and night, considering Stina was *Anglo* and Kam was a cousin of Kathra who had inherited almost the same deep blackness of skin. Erin joined them and powered the lock open. No cargo on this run, so nothing that required officials to check things off. Just four girls with money burning a hole in their pockets.

Kam triggered the hatch open and the four of them poured out onto the concourse. Erin took a moment to lock everything, just because, and stopped cold when she turned back.

They had a visitor Erin had missed when she stepped out.

That, or A'Alhakoth moved faster than a jack rabbit.

The blue youngster was standing directly across the way, like maybe she had been waiting more or less behind a pillar for a while and stepped out now.

Erin hadn't been paying that close of attention to the woman before, beyond her face and bones, so she took a moment to register the clothing. Plain. Almost drab. The sorts of pants and tunic you got from the remainder bin if you were lucky enough to find two unmatched that fit you.

Erin remembered those days.

A'Alhakoth was in a black that had been washed enough times to fade to gray. The belt was brown leather and didn't match anything, but looked like it might be an heirloom anyway. Possibly the only thing she had left from home as things wore out.

Poverty in deep space was a grinding, unforgiving bitch. That the Mbaysey had crawled far enough out of it to hire a personal chef was just a measure of the luck and patient skill of Kathra's and Yagazie's dream.

Erin started walking directly across, towards the newcomer. Behind her, she heard Iruoma shush the other two and then the three were probably in her wake. It was hard to tell over the usual background noise of any station: voices, footsteps, and music playing quietly in a vain attempt at soothing savage breasts.

Erin got close enough that they could talk, without getting right down in the tiny girl's face. And she was tiny. Only a meter and a half tall. At least half a head shorter than either Daniel or Ndidi, so that made her possibly the shortest adult person Erin had ever known. She'd been taller than that when she was eleven.

"Evening," Erin said companionably as she came to rest.

The girl didn't look as flighty today. Maybe had enough time to think about her options, and realize they were probably all bad from here.

Deep space was like that.

"Good evening," A'Alhakoth replied in Spacer in a voice somewhere between diffident and tough.

Little of both, maybe.

Erin studied her, waiting. The young woman had come to her, after all.

"Are you still recruiting?" the periwinkle pixie asked.

Erin had a hard time seeing someone that tiny as truly adult. Being blue didn't help.

"We are," Erin smiled wryly. "Still interested?"

"I am," the woman said. "What are the requirements?"

"Tonight, you go to dinner with us," Erin said, gesturing to the three women behind her and laughing to herself that Stina had come at the last moment.

She was the only *Anglo* in the comitatus, and one of only three who weren't old school Mbaysey from Tazo, before Yagazie had gotten the tribe off the reservation and into space. Central African Diaspora from Earth.

A'Alhakoth started to say something, but Erin cut her off.

"My treat on food," she said simply. "We're celebrating and having a little fun before we have to go back to work tomorrow."

"Thank you," the woman said carefully.

She wasn't dressed like the rest of them, so she would stand out, but at least there was a mix of skin tones tonight, like they would have with Daniel here. And he never wore anything remotely colored like the comitatus, cognizant that he was an outsider.

Even if he wasn't, anymore.

The girl's legs churned to keep up with the rest of them, since Stina was the next shortest and still had nearly thirty centimeters on her.

Erin kept them going through the darker areas and up to the nicer parts of the station. The tourist zones, where things were painted regularly. Plants and flowers in pots every three meters. Smiling faces.

At least she could tip someone under the table tonight and feel good about things.

Steak.

Daniel was fantastic at what he did, but they rarely got something like a good steak on *WinterStar*, even as the comitatus. Kathra had better ways to burn her money than that.

The woman seating them looked a little askance at the group of them being armed, but didn't say anything. Only half the people in here had obvious weapons, and Erin was planning on drinking somewhere else anyway.

"First things first," Erin said as the waiter took drink

orders and left menus. "I know more about you than you are aware, because I have a really good spy who found out things about you nobody should."

Those huge eyes got bigger as Erin watched. Girl stopped breathing as well. The others knew what was up, but everyone here was sworn life and soul to Kathra.

That included keeping a lot of secrets from outsiders like A'Alhakoth.

"Okay?" the young woman finally managed, grabbing her water and taking a drink to maybe wet a dry throat, and maybe to buy herself some time.

"So if you hadn't passed that check, you wouldn't be here now," Erin continued. "And that's saying a lot, because all of us are part of Kathra Omezi's comitatus. Her warriors."

"What does that mean?"

"The Mbaysey used to be economic slaves, back in the Sept Empire days a generation ago," Erin explained. "Kathra's mother got enough folks engaged that they changed the law and freed the slaves, but my grandma Ezinne still has this same mark on her face from where the masters tattooed her. Then Yagazie got the tribe to buy an old cargo starship and get into the trade business. Most of the menfolk had gone off to join the army or work in factories in those days and never came back, so the tribe was all women. Fifteen years ago, Yagazie Omezi had enough ships to move the entire tribe off the reservation at Tazo and we've never been based on a planet since."

"Are all her warriors women?" A'Alhakoth asked, looking around the table. "You had a male human with you before."

"He's actually Kathra's personal chef," Erin laughed along with the others. "But he's also a pretty good spy, you would just never understand that to look at him."

"Why are you telling me this?" the woman was twitchy again.

"Because he passed you," Erin said. "And I did as well, with what I learned from him. You're safe because you are honest. And a warrior in your own right. And in need. We might be able to help."

The kaniea woman blinked rapidly when surprised. Erin filed that away for future reference.

Too-Good-To-Be-True. That was the look she could see in the back of those navy blue eyes.

"What do you know of my quest?" the young woman asked now.

"Almost nothing," Erin replied, which was technically only a small lie, but she wanted to see how much the youngster would share with this group.

"My kind, the kaniea, are only recently space-born, having been uplifted by the anndaing four generations ago," she said with a nod to herself. Probably getting her ducks lined up for the first time in a while. "The culture is a complicated mix of iron age superstitions and galactic age technology unsure how to get along. In the old days, warriors were only admitted after they had undertaken a quest to prove their worthiness."

"Or to weed out the weak and stupid," Erin agreed. "We've seen that sort of thing ourselves."

"Just so," A'Alhakoth said with a nod. "The old woman told me I was to leave the world and seek my destiny, as it wasn't on Kanus."

"Are you a warrior?" Iruoma leaned in now and focused on the girl. Nobody had a scowl like Iruoma when she wanted to use it. The shaved head and cranial tattoos just amplified the effect.

"So I was trained, but I have four older brothers and a sister, so I will never inherit the title or the land. As best, I might be married off to a powerful nobleman if I proved myself worthy."

Erin joined the others in making rude noises at the thought of relying on a male for status.

What woman ever wanted to be kept?

"We don't bother with men," Erin said. "Except for the occasional tumble to scratch a weird itch. Eight tenths of the tribe are female. The four of us are warriors who protect the rest."

"Does your Commander Omezi need more warriors?" A'Alhakoth asked carefully, pressing her lips against each other when she was done.

"That's why we are having this conversation, A'Alhakoth ver'Shingi," Erin smiled at her. "You seem to have the heart. Do you have the skill and stomach to join us?"

"What do you do?" she asked, straightening now that they were all on something of a level ground. And apparently missing the part where Erin knew her full name, despite A'Alhakoth never sharing it.

Good spies, and all that.

"We serve Kathra's will," Erin said. "How we do that is what makes us warriors. We fight on the ground as well as fly combat Starfighters called Spectres, usually on patrol to protect the Tribal Squadron, and occasionally to fight with pirates or other fools."

"Would I even fit in a ship designed for someone your size?" she asked.

Erin laughed. Adanne Eguminyo could be convinced to modify a Spectre around a kaniea. All Erin had to do was bet her that is was impossible.

Engineers were the same, anywhere she'd ever been. Adanne would move the stars to prove her wrong.

"If you got to that part of your training, I have no doubt that we could make it work," Erin said. "Kathra only has twenty-two women plus herself in the comitatus right now because she is unwilling to relax her standards enough to allow others. How are you in ground combat?"

Those big blue eyes got cagey now. Back on safe ground, maybe.

"Sword, hammer, stick, poniard, bow, and six forms of unarmed combat," she smiled, as if challenging any of them to step out onto the dojo floor with her.

Erin had already decided to let Nkechi and Elyl have the first round at the woman, after watching memories of A'Alhakoth training.

Kaniean men were pretty much broad humans, which was weird considering how tiny this woman was, and she was largely representative of that gender.

"Firearms?" Kam asked now.

Kam was the deadshot in the comitatus. Erin only ever needed to hit close enough to center that a human would go down, dead or not on the first shot.

"Beams are extremely uncommon on Kanus," A'Alhakoth replied. "Gunpowder-charged slug-throwers were easier to make with our previous industrial base and that has remained with us even today. Above average as a hunter stalking large game. I've never had to kill someone with a gun."

Which suggested that she had killed people other ways, but neither Erin nor Daniel had spent that much time looking. Wasn't that important, once they understood the important parts about the youngster.

And if she could chase down large ungulates, or whatever equivalent Kanus had, she had to be good enough to stalk intelligent game, too.

The waiter returned now and distracted them with the food porn of describing all the different ways they could take their steaks and improve them, to the point Erin was positively drooling, but she had what she needed to know about A'Alhakoth ver'Shingi.

And where they were going, having a scout who had already traversed that same terrain outwards would be helpful.

There were likely to be some nasty customers in those sectors.

TWENTY-ONE

Daniel had never asked for these powers. Never wanted to be anything more than a chef. Still didn't want anything to do with them today, except there was nobody to give them away to.

Kathra or any of her comitatus would have taken them gladly, and done a better job than he could, but the power was gendered. Only males could use it.

The suit had continually reset itself to fit him as he had lost the last of his spare tire and gained leg muscles from working out more and having less stress in his life. He wore it pretty much continually now, under whatever pants and long-sleeve shirt the day called for.

Since Kathra kept the temperatures comfortable for her, he had to adjust the suit using the gem, and had added an extra piece of cloth so that the white light was not visible.

At least he was doing some good. More than just ending Urid-Varg as a conqueror and rapist of random women, as good as that was for the rest of the galaxy.

Each and everyone one of those little ships he had inherited on the Star Turtle were going to be sold, if they could, and the Mbaysey were reaping the rewards. They would be free.

Daniel wasn't sure he would ever be welcome back in the Sept Empire, even if he wanted to go back, since they would know who he had worked for. Worse, they might know that he controlled the Turtle, except they had not sent any assassins after him.

At least none he had recognized.

Something more than his imagination had touched him on three separate occasions now, so he couldn't just mark it down as paranoia or wishful thinking. Someone with a gem like his, only much smaller. Weaker, for lack of a better term.

Since Daniel didn't know how the mind magic of that *salaud* worked, he couldn't guess, except that they would not be able to take the Turtle away from him, if it came down to a contest of wills.

Assuming he fought them.

Whoever they were.

Daniel didn't know where Urid-Varg had gotten the Turtle. The oldest ghosts stayed deep in the darkness, unwilling to venture forth to talk to him. They just stared at him with damned, haunting eyes, as if daring him to banish them.

If he could…

Were Urid-Varg's enemies finally coming for him, unaware that he had died in the most embarrassing way possible? Who wanted to walk up to the gates of hell and explain that they'd been beaten to death by an angry cook with an empty fire extinguisher?

Nothing else made any sense, though. Hopefully, they would confront him at the end, rather than just launching a massive assault designed for the greater power Urid-Varg had been able to wield when he still existed on that damnable jewelry housing. If they would listen to reason, they might just turn out to be gendarmes, or something.

Or angry husbands, perhaps, considering some of the nightmares/memories Daniel had learned.

People with justification to do violence, even if they were aiming it at the wrong people.

Person.

Him.

Daniel looked around his quarters. Nothing had changed. He usually spent most of his time in the kitchen, or out front, feeding people or translating ancient books and memories into technical manuals and histories.

Even the addition of A'Alhakoth ver'Shingi to the crew didn't really change anything. He even knew where her kind came from, using newer memories than the K'bari who had fared so badly at Urid-Varg's hands.

Had he killed the K'bari, or just broken their will? Daniel couldn't tell from the memories, and some things simply did not translate from the culture of that ghost into terms Daniel could explain, let alone understand.

It was enough to know that the K'bari were no more as an organized nation, and possibly not even as a species, and that the timing coincided well with Urid-Varg's K'bari ghost.

How many xenocides had Daniel fallen heir to by taking Urid-Varg's place? Many of the ghosts would not talk to him, and he could not compel them without the conqueror's mental matrix and extra power behind it.

Just as well.

He didn't want to become a Mad God like that *salaud.*

Daniel took a deep breath and laid down on the bed. He had turned the lights down to a single notch above sleeping, so as to not distract, but to keep him awake as he worked. He stripped his pants and shirt off now, leaving only that annoyingly bright bodysuit that somehow acted like an organic spacesuit.

He sighed, remembering the first time he had awakened with memory of the power.

His gloves were on the end table he used as a nightstand. Those got pulled on, since he was intent on doing serious work tonight.

If someone was going to cause he or Kathra trouble, it would happen soon. The bulk of the tribal squadron had departed for points not discussed with outsiders. They would go off and do their harvesting in a little-known system for another week or three, until Kathra called them for a Concursion, once she got her new warship.

Tonight, he needed to search for other ghosts.

He could not listen for aliens. There were too many here, plus species he (and Urid-Varg) had never encountered. Such was the level of crossroads that Tavle Jocia represented.

The Sept might send an assassin to kill him and steal the gem, if they learned anything about how it worked. He didn't think Ugonna had told them. She hadn't known much at the point where Kathra had executed her. But the Sept were and always would be a risk.

The Free Worlds were a less organized place. They might have dealings with the sorts of pirates and criminals that would love to lay hands on a Star Turtle.

And someone with powers like his was hiding somewhere in this system. He had to find them.

Daniel closed his eyes and focused on his breathing. Some of his ghosts came out and watched. Most of them had quieted down, once they seemed to understand that he was the opposite of Urid-Varg in every way he could be.

Anything not to fall to the seductive call of evil.

But he needed power tonight. A good meal. No wine to

dull the senses. Not even a warm, beautiful woman lying next to him from which he could draw solace.

Areen might be a tough bad-ass outside this room, but he'd never lain with a better lover. And that said a lot, considering some of the groupies a top-rated chef encountered in his time.

Daniel opened his mind to the cosmos.

He wasn't trying to find anyone. There was nobody there, as far as he knew.

But they might leave holes he could locate.

He just had to push.

Nearby space was cold to the touch, but alive with the energy of the nearby star. Solar wind howled in frenzied, ionized tracks across the world around him. Gas giants answered in the distance. Space ships and stations yammered constantly on various radio waves.

All of it was background noise as he listened.

He turned his face to the station hanging nearby as *WinterStar* followed along in a trailing orbit of the planet. Those voices he knew. Human for the most part, just because they were at home and relaxed.

Aliens far from home tended to be uncomfortable here and kept their minds closed. A'Alhakoth had not been able to keep him at bay, but that was because he was focused on her and just across the table from her.

Were he trying to watch her from here, she would be invisible. Just another note in the cacophony.

He had to listen harder, just to try to pry out individual notes.

Or not.

Something caught his attention.

Or rather, nothing.

There was a hole in the voice of the station.

There.

In his mind, it was like someone had raised a hand to block the afternoon sun. He could still see around it and it left him almost blind, but there was a spot in the middle where nothing came through.

They had a shield that protected them from him.

Or something.

He didn't dare poke at it. They might have something that would notice his attempt. He didn't need to, anyway.

It was there.

He could see it, at least by the photo negative effect of something not being there.

He was too far away to isolate it. But he could fix that, next time he was on station. Erin and a few others should be with him. Possibly A'Alhakoth, since she was truly an alien around the humans. It would take the young woman a time yet to challenge them in the Spectres, but she was as good a warrior as they were, on the ground.

PART TWO
HUNTER

TWENTY-TWO

Comitatus dinner. Kathra looked around and confirmed that the hatch to the dining hall was closed.

All of her women were present. That included A'Alhakoth, the newest. She didn't fly a Spectre yet, but both Erin and Daniel had spoken in favor of her. And they'd seen the insides of her mind to judge. The outside was doing well also, for all her youth.

The kaniea, the woman had confirmed, aged slower than humans did. At twenty-two, she was perhaps the human equivalent of sixteen or seventeen, so a younger sister to Ndidi. About as mature as that woman, and Ndidi made a good role model, as she was accepted into the comitatus in spite of the fact that she would never fly.

A'Alhakoth just hadn't mastered the tools yet. Give her a year.

Kathra's newest warrior, now known as Spectre Twenty-Three, sat directly across from her, with Daniel and Ndidi on one side and Erin on the other. The kitchen was shut down and all the leftovers put away. Hot chocolate or fruit juice was all anyone was drinking tonight.

She fixed her eyes on A'Alhakoth and stared deep into the young woman's soul.

"Being in the comitatus is more than just being sworn into my service," she explained as those dark blue eyes locked on hers. "It means being privy to secrets that can never be told outside this room. Most of the crew know the general bits, but each of them have been tested and the disloyal removed."

"Or killed," the young woman said quietly.

"Or killed, yes," Kathra agreed. "Ugonna betrayed me and the entire Mbaysey over something petty. But small people plot small revenges. You have taken the oath, A'Alhakoth ver'Shingi."

"I have," Spectre Twenty-Three agreed.

"There is an inner secret you need to be aware of now," Kathra said, watching.

The young woman was still a stranger to most of the comitatus, even though she had spent a few weeks learning their ways. Daniel and Erin had walked her memories. Kam, Iruoma, and Stina had all taken her measure that first night and approved. The others had worked to incorporate her. None had found a reason to doubt her, other than youth, which they all had managed to make it through in their own time.

A'Alhakoth nodded carefully, probably afraid that the other shoe was going to drop now. It was, but not in a way that the woman could ever predict.

"A year ago, the Mbaysey were attacked by an alien," Kathra explained. "A powerful, ancient monster who had lived twelve thousand years and destroyed countless cultures in a broad path of destruction across the galaxy."

Those blue eyes narrowed. Perhaps she had heard legends of such a thing. Urid-Varg had not crossed anywhere near Kanus, but the K'bari had once been relative neighbors.

"He would have taken us all," Kathra continued. "Destroyed the Mbaysey and perhaps gone on to destroy all humans as well. We cannot know, although humans are a more warlike species than many he had encountered. Whether that would have saved them can never be known. We destroyed the beast."

Kathra turned to Daniel and smiled at him.

"Or rather, my cook did," she laughed.

A'Alhakoth's head snapped around to the *Rabic* male next to her. He smiled in a friendly, disarming way, still the softest, weakest person in the room without that gem to aid him.

"How?" the woman asked in genuine surprise.

"The Conqueror was looking for a new harem of women," Daniel replied quietly. "When he dominated all of the crew of *WinterStar* and the other vessels, he did not account for a male on this ship, so he missed me. That turned out to be a fatal mistake on his part."

"How?" she repeated absently, brow furrowed.

A'Alhakoth had only known Daniel as a cook and an intellect, not a warrior. Kathra knew the truth, though.

"I distracted him with a fire extinguisher," Daniel's smile grew a little lopsided as Kathra watched. "And then beat the *salaud* to death with it. But that wasn't the end of him."

"It wasn't?"

Yes, child. This is the other shoe. Take a deep breath and prepare for wonders and nightmares beyond any you have ever imagined.

"He had mental powers, and a backup plan," Daniel said. "A literal deadman switch, as it were. I was infected, and would have eventually fallen victim, but for the Commander."

Those blue eyes came back and around and studied her with new awe in them.

As they should. All women should live a little in awe of the Commander of the Mbaysey. Kathra smiled to reassure her and nodded for Daniel to continue.

"She was able to defeat and destroy him," Daniel grimaced now, but that was the memory of what it had taken out of him. What it took out of him daily. "I was able to steal some of his powers, and have put them to use for the Commander."

Sitting, he pulled his outer shirt off over his head, leaving only his pants and revealing the lime-green bodysuit with white stripes connecting to his extremities. That gem the size of her palm rested at the base of his throat, although it was connected directly now, rather than resting in that chrome and platinum setting.

It still pulsed with some inner fire as Kathra watched.

A'Alhakoth gasped.

"It can do many things," Daniel said in a voice trailing pain as Kathra listened, but she already knew that. "But there is one I need to show you now. May I take your hand?"

Kathra noted how the closest hand twitched, ever so slightly, but didn't withdraw.

A'Alhakoth turned to her for confirmation, and Kathra nodded.

"It's okay," Erin spoke up. "All of us have been there before you. And we will protect you."

That seemed to be the thing the traveler needed. Erin as a big sister.

She extended her hand and Daniel took it in his.

"Take a deep breath," he ordered her. "This will not hurt."

TWENTY-THREE

WHATEVER A'ALHAKOTH HAD BEEN EXPECTING when she took Daniel's hand, this was not it.

What had she been expecting?

"I work very hard to avoid evil and temptation," Daniel said.

They sat together in a room. A strange salon, with a large picture window and comfortable furniture. The sky out the window was the wrong color, almost the blue of her skin.

Daniel sat on the couch, with her in a chair at an angle to him. Everything seemed to be made of hand-crafted wood, lovely and well-made.

"Where are we?" she asked.

"Inside my mind," he replied. "I have learned to start here, and let people grow accustomed. Very little time is passing in the outside world while we talk."

"Why am I here?" A'Alhakoth demanded in a sharper voice.

She was a warrior, even before she had met Kathra Omezi and her comitatus. Before she had taken the third set of vows. She did not rise, but did prepare her muscles for combat.

"The gem gave me mental powers that no other human has," he said quietly. "Very few species have, in fact. The Commander and the others have been here, and seen what you are about to see, but they are human. I wanted a moment for you to adjust before we take the next step."

"Where are we going?" she asked, voice still sharp, but relaxing.

Daniel Lémieux was taking visible pains to not present as a threat. He might yet be a wolf in sheep's clothing, but she could take care of herself.

"In order to understand, you have to become me," he explained. "Erin had me do something similar when she first met you, using my powers to study your mind, even as you were unaware of the violation. I must apologize for that. I was working under her orders. Right now, you and I are still seated at the table across from the Commander. No time has passed. Are you ready for the next step?"

"I am," A'Alhakoth decided, whatever it was.

She fell into a pit. There was no other way to describe the feeling of falling a great distance, as tall buildings surrounded her.

Eventually, she hovered in the air. Buildings stretched to the horizon in all directions as she turned.

The air had a smell. Rich and nutty, like a forest just after a fall rain, as the mushroom crop is ready to be harvested and the ground itself was damp and squishy under her boots.

She studied the building closest to her and reached out a hand. Suddenly, she was standing before a bookcase like one her father kept, lined to the top with a variety of tomes.

A'Alhakoth pulled a book down and opened it.

Genarde.

It was a planet deep in the distant Sept Empire, on the far side of the Free Worlds. Daniel had come from there.

She found herself standing in the kitchen of *Pain du Soir*, a bistro Daniel had owned. The air tasted of freshly baked bread, with a hint of quiet despair underneath.

Across the busy room, humans worked with heads down and occasional barks at each other as they assembled meals and delivered them to the front for paying customers. Her hands were preparing a ratatouille, although she wasn't sure how she knew that.

Or even knew what a ratatouille was.

Daniel's hands were stirring the simmering sauce slowly, except that they were her hands, *Rabic* brown instead of a more natural periwinkle. The sauce was perfect as they tasted it with a carved wooden spoon like her mother might have used, back on Kanus.

She watched herself add the vegetables and broth to a broad baking dish made of glass, and then add a layer of already cooked ground meat over the top before sprinkling shredded cheese and sliding the entire mess into a nearby stove to turn into magic.

A taste of home.

But not her home. His.

These were his memories. That was his Golden Diamond on the wall, marking the first stage of utter, gustatory excellence, one of only four such restaurants in that entire sector of space so honored.

She was Daniel Lémieux right now. Those books were his memories. She was surrounded entirely by his life.

"What would you like to know?" his disembodied voice asked.

"Why this memory?" she looked up at the ceiling and asked.

"That was perhaps the last time I was happy," he said.

"Tomorrow, Angel ruins everything, but tonight, the ratatouille variant came out so perfect that I still come here to savor it."

She saw Angel. Saw the night Daniel had had enough and sold his restaurant for whatever cash his *Sous Chef* had in his wallet. Saw Daniel walk away and never look back, not even with a hint of regret.

"Show me the monster," she commanded.

There was a moment of vertigo, and A'Alhakoth found herself on the main repair deck of *WinterStar*. All of the crew was lined up, eyes unseeing with an inner glow as a strange, alien creature ordered them to strip, that he might pleasure himself on their unresisting bodies.

She felt rage deep inside herself, but the wave of anger from Daniel was like a mountain falling down, destroying everything in its path.

Commander Omezi had already been reduced to a victim. The others were following.

She covered Urid-Varg's face with foam and watched him cough and gag, before she bashed him again and again, splattering blood and brains everywhere in her wrath.

His fury.

That was Daniel she was feeling. Daniel's fury at what that *violeur* planned. His response to someone taking instead of asking.

He would always ask. And take no for an answer with no hard feelings. She did not have to fear for herself with the only man on the ship.

A'Alhakoth grabbed other memories at random. Cooking on *WinterStar*. Cooking on Genarde, in all of the kitchens he had known. Flying through space.

The Star Turtle.

Holy shit.

"Yes," Daniel said. "That is the most terrible secret. The

one we must keep from everyone. The Mbaysey know. The Sept is aware, but has not come to understand my secrets, or Kathra's. It is power, A'Alhakoth."

She turned, looking around the endless stacks of books, but could not find the man she wanted to confront.

Suddenly, they were both back in that room, seated like someone would be delivering tea shortly.

"You did that to me," she accused. "Ransacked my memories without permission."

He nodded.

They were gone again, back to that day she met Erin. A'Alhakoth was staring at herself across a small gap, with Erin between them, facing her, even as she watched another A'Alhakoth across from her.

She was Daniel. He had done these things.

She climbed into her own mind with him and looked around. Returned a moment later when Erin ordered it, and watched that woman go much deeper into who she was and why she was here, trying to solve the mystery of who the blue girl was studying them across the food court.

Even from here she could smell her own desperation to escape the onset of poverty, in a place where men might make terrible demands. A woman might as well, but it wouldn't be as bad, she had hoped.

But the quest had carried her as far as it could. She couldn't have even made it home easily at that point.

And then Erin found her. Daniel was just a passive observer as she looked around both of them, him and his memories of being Erin in that moment.

All of the women had been Daniel. Had been inside his mind, just as she was inside his now. He had brought her here so that she would understand.

A man's word were just that. Words. Promises could be

kept or broken. Honored or ignored. Lies you could not discern until it was too late.

Except she had seen to the core of Daniel Lémieux. Read his soul, his heart, his mind.

A'Alhakoth could not envision what kind of man would be granted that sort of power, and then not use it. Not conquer with it.

So he showed her.

He called it the Left Hand Of Evil.

With that sort of power you could just shut a woman's mind down while you ravaged her body. Or leave her awake as a passive witness, screaming in her mind but trapped in her flesh and unable to fight back. When that got boring, that level of power made it possible to make her participate with an appearance of willingness.

And if you were really a rapist, perhaps make her enjoy it.

Finally, you could make her *dependent* on it.

Evil itself.

That was the fear she tasted at the core of the man. That he would cross some line, even accidentally, and end up there, changing someone into someone else, when there was nothing they could do to stop him.

She saw nightmares where he turned the Star Turtle into the face of a nearby sun and leapt to his death, taking the gem and all that power with him, rather than allowing someone else to grasp it.

In some of the dreams, he was an old man. In others, no older than the one who had sat next to her at dinner.

"You understand?" he asked finally.

"I do," A'Alhakoth replied gravely.

His fear wasn't for himself, but for the ones around him, and what he might do to them in a fit of pique. Or the lengths to which he might go, if he felt it was necessary to protect Kathra Omezi and her comitatus.

Including the newest member.

A'Alhakoth suddenly found herself back in her own body, seated in the dining hall with Daniel on one side and Erin on the other. Kathra Omezi sat across from her with a compassionate face.

They had all been through this particular fire. Only Kathra had killed with that power.

A'Alhakoth remembered to breathe.

"Now," Kathra nodded. "Now you are mine."

TWENTY-FOUR

The fools had chosen to fight.

Naupati Pasdar laughed, but only in his mind. Outwardly, he maintained a stern scowl as he watched the base implode and the few junkyard Starfighters still surviving turn and flee in different directions on their pitiful valence drives.

They would be no threat to anyone if they did manage to escape, wherever they landed.

He had broken them.

A Septagon was the most perfect weapon ever devised for destroying pirate bases on small moons. The target could not flee.

One merely had to align the bow of the ship with the target and annihilate it.

Even planets protected by atmospheres could not shelter a city from the Axial Megacannon.

The moon in front of him was in the process of disintegrating, ending the pirate base, and any threat from the people there.

Pasdar didn't care who they were. This system was

marked uninhabited on even the most recent gazetteer, so they were squatters in a system where he needed to build his next base. Pasdar didn't even need the moon, which was why he could destroy it. Just solitude to build a base.

Had the locals been legitimate businessmen, they would have known better than to scramble a dozen or so armed tugboats to engage sixty Patrol craft and a Septagon.

Pasdar assumed he had just done the galaxy a favor by destroying a band of pirates, not that the Free Worlds would appreciate the effort. It would cost them one of their systems, and establish a place where the Sept had a salient thrust deep into their territory.

Someone would find it eventually. They might even complain, but Pasdar was planning to leave four Patrols here for now, while sending messages home requesting enough forces be assigned to this system to hold it against most future threats. The Free Worlds could still dislodge him, if they chose, since Vorgash would be moving on, an unstoppable iceberg working its way deeper into the trade lanes.

Soon, the task would become even more dangerous. The authorities would discount a few pirates with wild tales of a Septagon destroying their base. Eventually, his Patrols would begin to encounter other ships, and the word would get out.

He wondered if Kathra Omezi would understand that he was coming for her. That it was time for her experiment in social justice, or whatever she called it, to be crushed, lest others draw the conclusion that they could thumb their noses at the Lords of the Sept.

She would need to be made an example of.

Six Patrols would have made shorter work of that, but he had to consider that *thing*.

That *Star Turtle*.

It had apparently feared the Axial Megacannon, even as it

resisted the Ram Cannons on Uwalu. He would need a Septagon to kill it, presumably.

Or at least break whatever ties it had with Omezi and her people. Without that, she could be hounded until she surrendered or died. Either outcome was acceptable, since it would convey the correct message to the rest of the galaxy.

You will not resist the Sept Empire.

Rostami stood from his command chair and approached where Amirin stood at the front of the space. Not diffidently, but perhaps carefully, mindful that Pasdar had fallen silent at the front of the Great Causeway, staring at the cooling cloud of debris and plasma that had been a pirate base until very recently.

Pasdar turned to him with a frosty smile and a nod.

"All resistance has ended, Naupati," Rostami said professionally.

Just in case Pasdar had doubts, in the aftermath of the Axial Megacannon.

"Arrest any survivors," Pasdar ordered. "Question them and then execute any you credibly believe to be pirates. The rest can be sent to work farms back home for reeducation."

He turned and stared into the darkness, as though he could pierce it with his mind and locate Kathra Omezi across however many light-years.

"Begin construction of Forward Operating Base Ardabil," Pasdar continued. "You and I will review contingency plans later, but we will need to send a courier home tomorrow with updates and requests for additional Patrol forces in this system. Prepare for an extended stay here while we fortify the place. In two weeks, I expect to proceed with the next phase."

TWENTY-FIVE

KATHRA WATCHED Isaev's docks in the distance out her personal cabin's window, moving slowly as *WinterStar*'s disk rotated around its central hub. She had moved her ship to a point midway between the TradeStation and Isaev's graving yard, the massive factory station where new ships took form.

The work was nearly done over there, faster than most people had probably expected, but she wasn't spending money for unnecessary extravagances inside the hull. No grav field inducers, nor the massive power systems they required. No extra effort inside to hide raw steel plates that made up the hull. Not even carpeting that would wear out and have to be replaced regularly.

The Mbaysey lived rough, stoic lives. At least the folks on *WinterStar* and the new ship. ClanStar inhabitants could spend time and energy on making things softer and prettier for themselves, but the warriors did not.

That let her build a new ship quickly. She would need it.

Already, Kathra was nervous about the amount of time she had spent at Tavle Jocia, nearly two months, when her normal TradeStation visit was a matter of two to three days.

Just long enough to order new supplies, deliver trade materials, and depart again once she loaded up.

Daniel had a plan to investigate the station for the pixies that he was convinced were following him. Or her. She had told him flatly that he was not allowed to even begin his looking until the new ship was done and she was in the process of acceptance trials with the builders.

If he was provoking someone who had been content to just watch up until now, she wanted to be ready to flee at the moment something went wrong.

With her new ship.

The Sept had spies here, reporting back to their masters. Getting a message out of the Free Worlds and drawing trouble to Tavle Jocia was a longer round trip than she was going to be here, so Kathra generally ignored them, except to have Daniel inspect every new candidate.

A knock at the door drew her eyes from the window and Kathra brought herself back to today's problems, rather than what might lurk around some distant corner.

She walked to the door and opened it, smiling down at A'Alhakoth as the young woman stood at attention.

It had been an interesting challenge, dressing her in the tangerine and black that was the current uniform of the comitatus. Nobody was used to making clothing that small, so they had had to create entirely new patterns by cutting one of the woman's existing outfits into pieces.

Not that she had probably missed the old faded grays, almost on the verge of disintegrating.

"Come in," Kathra stepped back and gestured.

Her newest warrior entered, perhaps a bit hesitantly, but Kathra directed her to one of the two chairs and closed the hatch again.

Like her warriors, Kathra lived a rough life. She liked to occasionally think of herself as a barbarian warlord in the distant past of Mother Earth, living in a tent, rather than a palace.

Her personal cabin was no larger than Erin's. Or A'Alhakoth's for that matter. Three meters wide. Five deep. Two footlockers in a corner and a dresser. Two chairs. A bed that two people would find uncomfortable for sleeping. Nightstand. Porthole currently pointed at the TradeStation, with the graving yard coming back soon.

At not quite two revolutions per minute, *WinterStar* had the appearance of planetary gravity, without the expense of grav field inducers.

Any way she could reduce her operating costs.

"You're wondering why I asked you here," Kathra stated as she took the other chair, not quite close enough to touch knees and angled apart thirty degrees. Comfortable, when her office might have sent the wrong message and wound the woman up all the wrong ways.

A'Alhakoth nodded, entirely compact in her surface emotions tonight.

"I am going to send you on a mission shortly," Kathra said. "It is not secret from Daniel or Erin, but you will be operating separate from the rest of the comitatus, and undercover."

Again, the nod, a little more confident this time. Like the young woman could see the logic of an alien pretending to not be part of the comitatus, if nobody outside the ship knew the truth. Station authorities knew, because Kathra had added the woman to her crew officially, but the average person would just see her as another kaniea. There were a few men of the species on the station, but no other women that Kathra was aware of.

Or Daniel was aware of, and he had looked at her request.

"Understood, Commander," A'Alhakoth said firmly.

"Daniel and Erin will be looking for trouble," Kathra said. "You will go over early and just fade into the background. Nobody in the comitatus will apparently know you while you are gone, but you have a skyvox that can be used to contact us, and us you."

"Do we know what Daniel is looking for?" she asked.

Kathra had seen the woman surface from living inside Daniel's memories, but it was different every time, and for every woman.

We each of us are not the people we were yesterday.

"Not even Daniel knows," Kathra said. "His theory is that someone was chasing Urid-Varg, and that was why the man had not stopped anywhere to conquer himself another empire in a long time. He was afraid of them, whoever they were. I have no idea who or what they might be, but Daniel is convinced that something is on the TradeStation right now, and that they are a threat."

"When do we begin?" A'Alhakoth asked, matter of fact.

Yes, the youngest daughter of a relative nobleman from a culture that had not given up all the trappings of their barbarous history, in spite of access to space. Long-lived and slow-growing, they might never impact the rest of the galaxy with some of their militant ethos, but Kathra could make use of a daughter with no great reason to go home soon.

"You begin with the next cargo run to the TradeStation," Kathra said. "You will return to your civilian clothing, and some we will make up for you. Erin will transport you, and once you slip out of the SkyCamel, you are on your own until we need you, or you contact us. Questions?"

"The mental powers are from the gem?" she asked. "Daniel had none before that?"

"Correct," Kathra said. "Humans have always claimed to have some level of abilities in that field, but nothing that science has been able to confirm, or replicate. The gem acts as a repository of many things, including raw power, and keys to his mind. You will kill any male that gets hold of that power other than Daniel, if you can."

"If I can?"

Those eyes got big. Bigger. Eyeslits popped open a moment later to reinforce the image.

"If he knows an attack is coming, nothing hand-held can hurt him," Kathra said. "That is part of the reason he is always at such pains to let me and the others into his mind, so we can remind him to stay human."

"What is the alternative?" A'Alhakoth asked.

"Urid-Varg saw himself as a god," Kathra said. "A mad, angry, rapist fool of a god, who could do anything he wanted because nobody could stop him. His arrogance was his undoing. Daniel would rather kill himself than go down that road."

"I see," she nodded. "How long until he does lose control? Or at least interest in helping the Mbaysey achieve their destiny?"

"Years, I hope," Kathra said. "Again, there is nothing we can do to stop him, except provide him the same sort of refuge you have found. That anchor of sanity will keep him here, until it is no longer effective. I can only hope that he departs on happy terms at that point, rather than flying through the flaming wreckage of the Tribal Squadron on his way elsewhere."

A'Alhakoth gulped. Good. That meant she had the beginning of wisdom, to see the road Kathra had chosen for herself and her people.

Kathra saw the young woman out with instructions to talk to Erin and organize everything, while she went back to the window and watched her future slowly slide by, over there.

This was not the easy road. But Yagazie had seen the

future, and gathered up all the women at Tazo and bought a starship. Trade had bought a second and a third. Eventually, they had left Tazo entirely and danced at the edges between Sept and Free Worlds.

The Sept Empire had not been able to stop her. Maybe they would send assassins now, like they had done to Yagazie.

She just had to stay ahead of them, until they couldn't ever find her again.

TWENTY-SIX

THE SKYCAMEL WAS DOCKED and Daniel felt the weight of his mission descend on him like a rainstorm before he could unbuckle the straps. He sat still for a moment and tried to remember how to breathe.

"You okay?" Erin asked from the pilot's seat.

"Dancing with visions of failure and mortality," he said as he turned to her.

"Kill them first, then," she offered, rising.

Erin was like that. Every problem was just an excuse to go sideways and find another way around it. Or use brute force to destroy it.

Daniel was already skidding sideways on ice, careening down a hill and waiting to slam into something at the bottom, but he had brought it upon himself, so he wasn't about to complain now. He had chased after those ghosts, after all.

They had mostly avoided him except for that first touch, and a few since that might have been unguarded moments. Or they might have been his imagination.

But he could not let the mystery go. It was like eating a

new dish and spending all night unraveling the tastes so he could replicate the recipe in his head.

"You coming?" Erin asked, so he finished unbuckling and rose.

Iruoma, Kam, and Nkechi were already waiting at the airlock for him, dressed in their combat finest and ready for whatever might occur.

Erin had brought Kam and Nkechi for their lethal skills. Daniel had insisted on Iruoma for her scowl. Erin was there to supervise and keep him out of trouble. Somewhere, A'Alhakoth was hiding, waiting to be their ace in the hole if they needed her.

But Daniel was already on his own.

In the darkness, Kathra was supervising the last of the efforts to move things from *WinterStar* to the new warship, which she had called SeekerStar. They were keeping *WinterStar*, but Kathra would hide it someplace else for now, once they had moved everything.

Kathra lacked the crew to have both ships running, without draining all of the ClanStars of staff that were needed to keep the tribe fed.

They would recruit more warriors and sailors later.

Iruoma put her hand on his shoulder and smiled. She had a warm smile when she forgot to scowl angrily at the universe. He drew strength from her touch as Erin opened the hatch and stepped out onto the main deck of the concourse.

"Thoughts?" Erin asked.

"Burgers," Daniel said. "I skipped lunch for an excuse to sit quietly in a restaurant on station and think."

Kam led. Apparently she knew a joint off the main walkway, kind of hidden, like the place where they had first found A'Alhakoth. Something for station folks, rather than spacers. Although the smart spacers learned to find these places and generally keep quiet about them.

Daniel was in the middle, standing as usual at the bottom of a bowl of mountains from the taller women around him. Both Iruoma and Nkechi had eight centimeters on him, and Nkechi was built like a Forceball Middle Wing, back on Genarde. Her arms were as big as his thighs, and her shoulders always felt like they were a meter across.

Hopefully, they would be enough. He wasn't sure anything would be.

Still, they got him to a burger joint that had apparently been a Polynesian themed place in an earlier incarnation, with bamboo and thatch decorations and South Pacific art painted on various surfaces.

Daniel almost missed the thought of what the place might have once been, but the smell of grease and fried meat coming from the back was enough promise to make his stomach rumble with excitement.

"So what are we looking for?" Kam asked forthrightly, staring at him from a level that always made him jump.

Sitting, all of the women were his height, because they were all legs. He didn't have to be the smallest person in the room. Good for his psyche to remember that.

"I don't know," Daniel reminded her. It wasn't like they hadn't had this conversation on the ship four hours ago. "We're going hunting, and hopefully I can find them. After that, I hope they'll talk to me. If not, I brought all of you to save me."

That got a round of laughs. All of these women considered themselves tougher than any *male* they would ever encounter. Daniel didn't want to remind them that Urid-Varg had never encountered humans in the flesh until he boarded *WinterStar* looking for a harem.

He could only imagine what whoever it was hunting Urid-Varg might be.

His stomach was too rumbly to concentrate, so Daniel ordered the basic burger and fries, plus an Italian soda made with sweet cherry and cream. It was a nostalgic touch of home that took him to a first date when he was sixteen.

A last date, too, when she had ended up horrified and offended at his dream to cook. Another one like Angel that probably ended up as a groupie chasing Forceball players until she was too old.

He smiled and looked around.

Burgers were apparently a thing across species, if your digestion could handle it. Or the food here was that good. Only midafternoon and the place was nearly full. Three-quarters human by occupancy, but that was much lower than he would have expected, even on this TradeStation.

He listened to the ribald conversation around him without really participating. Areen was the only one who ever shared his bed. Yejide, Spectre Eleven, had a tremendous crush on him, but was held back by her shyness on that one topic, and a respect that Areen might have staked a claim.

Daniel didn't feel like an object, but he could see where Yejide was trapped. He couldn't say anything to her without admitting how deep he had peeked. Others in the comitatus had either missed those memories, or chosen not to say anything to either of them on the topic.

Only Ndidi knew.

Maybe he needed to walk up to Yejide and say something, one of these days. But that could wait. He hoped.

Instead of adding to the pile of dirty jokes, Daniel closed his eyes and let his senses expand outward. He couldn't reach far without pulling on the gloves and really concentrating, but a good chunk of the station itself was within his range right now.

He pushed, listening for silence instead of minds. The waste reclamation systems were huge and below him, so he could account for that space. Similarly, the battery arrays that kept the inhabitants in power from the sun-sensitive skin of the station itself.

Grav Field Inducers were huge, especially when you had to cover whole lobes of a TradeStation. Those took up two entire decks that could have each held a SkyCamel standing on its nose.

Where else?

He was reminded of the ancient literary reference to solving a mystery by proving that the dog didn't bark. Silence was suspect, but not definitive. There might not be anybody there to think or dream.

But most of those places were small, and irregularly shaped. What he had seen when he looked before was a perfect sphere of silence, uninterrupted by thought.

There were a few places above him.

He leaned back and looked at the thatched roof overhead, as if his eyes could pierce the decks to see, but they remained proof.

"Dinner," Erin poked him quietly as the waitress delivered plates of food.

He must have been gone longer than he thought, if they'd had long enough to cook.

"Eat," Erin said quietly as he came back to himself. "Then we'll talk."

TWENTY-SEVEN

Erin paid attention to Daniel, even as the other three were focused on immediate threats. She saw his eyes get big and then small, as he concentrated on something overhead. He had been gone so long that she had to wake him up when food arrived.

They ate in relative silence, companionable as everyone consumed pretty good burgers.

Once the waitress removed plates, Erin studied Daniel's face closer.

"Did you find them?" she asked.

"No," he slumped. "But I think I might know where to look."

"The upper decks?" Erin asked, guessing based on earlier. "Permanent housing rather than transient?"

"It might not be enough that they are looking for me," Daniel replied. "They may be waiting for me to lead them to the Turtle."

"So they could destroy it?" Iruoma leaned in.

"Or both of us," Daniel turned to her. "I don't know where Urid-Varg got it. None of the ghosts remember that far back. At least not the ones willing to talk to me. It's possible he stole it somewhere along the line and they want it back."

"Didn't you say it was alive?" Kam asked now, her hair cropped even closer than the normal one centimeter halo she normally wore. Today, it was almost as short as Iruoma's shaved head.

"Indeed," he agreed. "Slowly consuming things like the ClanStars and *ForgeStar* do, but in the case of the Turtle, it lives off such things, and grows extremely slowly."

"So it will get even bigger?" Kam pursued the thought.

"It already has," Daniel said. "It grows perhaps one millimeter a year right now, but I don't know if it is adult, or just that old. The person who knew is probably dead, and I'm hoping these aren't gendarme come to arrest me for possession of stolen goods."

Erin smiled along with the rest of the women. Accessories to the crime, perhaps, but those stolen goods were upgrading the Tribal Squadron to something that could perhaps resist even ambitious pirates and local navies that wished to challenge the Mbaysey.

It would be even more interesting once both *WinterStar* and SeekerStar were fully operational. Erin could only imagine the power of eighty or more Spectres flying in a massive formation, escorting the two warships into some sort of combat.

Not enough to defeat a Septagon, but probably enough to annihilate a couple of Patrols, if the fools didn't immediately flee from Kathra Omezi.

"So where do we go now?" she asked Daniel, falling back on practical needs.

"Up," Daniel replied. "I need to find a spot where I can sit quietly in the middle of the inhabitant deck and look. I can see nothing now, but they might be hiding, or they might have left. And they might be figments of my imagination, but I need to prove that the dog did not bark."

"You are a weird man, Daniel Lémieux," Nkechi smiled at him.

"*Oui*," he smiled back. "Keeps things from getting boring."

"In light of the last year or so, perhaps boring would not be the worst outcome?" she fired back at him.

"Trying, *mademoiselle*," he said.

Erin paid and they departed. They remained all the way around Daniel as escorts, but he had to direct her, heading the group into an elevator that took them to a promenade largely dedicated to locals. It wasn't off-limits to spacers, but didn't have much in the way of shops, and those were more focused on the needs of someone living on the station, like a green grocer and a library filled with actual books, rather than electronic versions you could buy for storage in your devices to keep you entertained between stations.

Erin didn't have a library card for Tavle Jocia TradeStation, and didn't feel like going through the process of getting one, so she found a bench nearby and sat Daniel down. The other three spread out a little, but Erin sat down next to him, mostly to keep him from falling over if he got too lost in himself.

"Go," she ordered him. "We've got you here, and I can always tackle you again if you lose your mind."

They shared a quick grin at that. Urid-Varg had snuck up on him sleeping and taken over. Areen had followed and called for help, and Erin had bounced him off a deck, breaking the monster's hold long enough for Daniel to tell Kathra what she needed to do to kill the beast and free Daniel.

At least as free as he would ever get.

Erin opened her skyvox and sent a coded pulse outwards.

She had no idea where the newest member of the comitatus was hiding, but A'Alhakoth needed to know that they were hunting so she could stalk with them.

She wasn't sure what the young woman might be able to do, but any surprise would help Erin twist a bad situation to her advantage.

TWENTY-EIGHT

THERE WERE beads of sweat at his browline and his palms were clammy, but Daniel swallowed past his sudden fear and tried to breathe regularly.

He didn't know why he was doing this. It would have been just as easy to pretend nothing was wrong and flee the station with the Commander, once she had enough big guns to stop anybody chasing them.

Except he knew that SeekerStar was going to be just as powerless against whoever they were as *WinterStar* had been against Urid-Varg. Those mental powers didn't care how thick the steel plates were that protected your hull. Or how far a Ram Cannon could range to damage someone.

They crept in on you at night, when you thought to sleep, bringing terrible dreams.

Urid-Varg would have been like that, Daniel realized as his butt warmed the seat beneath him. The Conqueror might have chosen to take all of humanity under his control, or at least the key elements.

Humans were still young in galactic terms. The K'bari

had gotten old and perhaps a little senescent by the time they met their doom, but humans were still full of fight.

In Daniel's worst nightmares, he saw himself as some sort of messiah figure, unleashing his forces on an unsuspecting galaxy and ruling over everything with his human governors.

It wouldn't last. They never did. But he could enjoy a few centuries of utter control in the meantime. Urid-Varg had only learned that lesson about failure later, after enough of his empires had washed away like sand castles under his feet.

Daniel closed his eyes and leaned enough of his weight against Erin to reassure himself that he wasn't alone.

He reached inside himself and leapt outwards.

Perhaps he was closer. Perhaps it was finally time for the confrontation they had been engineering. Maybe it was just luck, but Daniel could not identify the good or bad that came with it.

A space of darkness appeared in the middle of his vision. In the past, he had seen a station like this as something akin to a school of fish, or perhaps a swarm of fireflies. Bright lights swirling around.

Something.

There was a hollow spot, perfectly spherical. He wasn't at the edge of it, but he could see it clearly enough. Lights approaching the edge of it vanished when they crossed that line, while others appeared from within, as if people walking out of darkness to arrive at the edge of a streetlight.

Daniel left his body behind and orbited the sphere, always remaining a considerable distance back, lest they somehow detect the effect of his approaching. It felt organic, in ways he could not adequately describe.

Soft and pliable, rather than the rigidity of glass or steel. Wavering a little, back and forth, as if the surface was actually a pond and a bird had just landed, sending out tiny ripples that wobbled away.

It felt cold, though, rather than warm. Like it would suck all the heat out of his body if he touched it. A machine would feel warm, generating such a field and projecting it.

Daniel returned to his body and flinched as he awoke from whatever dreams he had possessed. Erin was still next to him. Fortunately, he hadn't started to drool on her just yet.

He sought a map of the station in his memory and compared that to the place he had just been.

"Lobe two," he muttered as he righted himself.

"The alien wing," she replied, just as quietly.

"*Oui*," Daniel nodded and started to rise, slowly lest his head fall off. "They are not human, but we already knew that. This just confirms that they are even less so than I thought."

Erin stood quicker and caught him just as he was about to pitch over forwards.

"Are you okay to do this?" she asked. "It looks like it has taken more out of you than it should have."

"That's just the fear, Erin," he said, staring up at her face and noting the concern hidden carefully in the back of her eyes. "If I don't do this now, I might never work up the courage to try again. If you think it might be too dangerous, the four of you could withdraw and return to SeekerStar."

It wasn't meant to be a low blow. He wasn't sure there was much they could do, besides keep him from falling over, but these women were warriors of Kathra's comitatus. They would see such a thing as cowardice, so Erin growled at him, stood him upright again, and nodded to the others.

Five of them, walking into hell perhaps.

At least he wouldn't be alone.

TWENTY-NINE

HER NEW SKYVOX beeped quietly as A'Alhakoth read a history of the recent Sept Empire, written from the perspective of the Free Worlds, who didn't have any particular reason to view their neighbor as a patriotic fighter for human rights and liberty, like the Sept liked to see themselves.

The Free Worlds had chosen to integrate humans with non-humans, mixing freely in their colonies and their laws, unlike the Sept, who maintained a rigid caste system that was baked directly into their entire legal system.

As a tribe of Central African Diaspora—and A'Alhakoth understood what that meant now—the Mbaysey were near the bottom of the ladder, all the more so because they were a matriarchal society almost as extreme as one could get.

The only thing that could be worse, as far as the Persians ruling the Sept Empire were concerned, would be an alien woman seeking legal rights.

No, that wasn't true. She was at least close enough to pass for human if the lights were dim. There were others, like the

Vida, that were probably rated lower than a Sept *Vuzurgan*'s prize stallions and camels, if push came to shove.

A'Alhakoth was astonished and insulted by such behavior, but it really wasn't much different from her homeworld, when she really thought about it. The Sept just had the benefit of ruling thousands of worlds, rather than all of one and small parts of two others.

But her vox caused her to close the reader and mentally prepare herself. Erin had sent a message earlier that her team was hunting, so A'Alhakoth was dressed, prepared, and almost hyper.

This new message narrowed things down. Daniel had apparently found a lead. Or a sign.

A'Alhakoth checked her gear and confirmed everything. Cheap clothing in that universal gray that everyone at the bottom of the social and economic ladder seemed to wear. Hair tied was tied back today, rather than the complicated braids she normally wore.

Hopefully, the look would convey vulnerability to humans encountering her. Non-threatening.

Anything that might let her get close enough to get to someone with hands or a small club.

She wasn't bringing blades or firearms today. Again, non-threatening. And she didn't know what information Daniel or Erin might require, so she needed to be able to take someone down hard but not kill them.

At least not immediately.

She situated everything in their appropriate pockets, and looked back into the room where she had been staying. Humans called them coffins, but she was a smaller scale, so it was just crowded, rather than psychologically oppressive. A'Alhakoth made her way to the door on hands and knees and exited.

The place was cheap enough. Low profile, for someone

hanging on precariously to the lowest rung of society. There had been offers of companionship in the last few days. Even offers to pay for such things. A'Alhakoth had only had to beat someone up once before everyone became much more polite.

She looked all the way around her before moving on and confirmed that she was alone as she locked the hatch and took a breath. Six stacks of six coffins, one atop the other like a square insect hive with catwalks across the front leading to stairs on her right.

Erin had said Lobe Two. A'Alhakoth was familiar with that area, but had never stayed there. It was dedicated to non-standard environments, for aliens uncomfortable with the rest of the station, whether that was too hot, too cold, or the wrong gravity. A few places even had the ability to maintain entirely separate atmospheres, if you needed certain things to breathe, or not breathe.

Hopefully, whoever it was Daniel was chasing was just hiding over there, safer because you could remain in your own area.

A'Alhakoth didn't want to think about what monsters might lurk on those decks.

THIRTY

It was nearly done. Kathra stood on the bridge of her new CommandStar and smiled. Ifedimma *Ife* Ogu and her women were hard at work in the zero-gravity space, triple-checking everything, but they were happy.

Larger, faster, tougher, meaner than *WinterStar* and ready to take the tribe into a new future. Hopefully, one where the Sept would not pursue her. Perhaps no one would be able to follow her, because she was never going to be tied even to a star nation again.

Daniel had done much to ensure that future, handing her the four ships for sale to a collector like the man standing next to her, and promising to return later with at least half of the rest for a future sale.

WinterStar had been a little packed, carrying twenty-three Spectres and the four alien craft. SeekerStar could take the whole load and still have plenty of space left on the flight deck.

New ClanStars? New *WinterStars*?

What could she do with a larger tribe?

"I take it that the ship meets with your approval,

Commander?" Trade Factor Isaev asked with a knowing smile. He was standing to one side with his feet hooked under a bar and one hand holding a post for people who didn't have a seat to buckle into, like Ife and her crew.

The man was also alone save for his majordomo, with several members of the comitatus providing security here on the bridge. Everyone was aboard SeekerStar finally, save for a skeleton crew on *WinterStar* to maintain systems.

"It does," Kathra replied.

She didn't like the man one bit, but he had been a relatively honest businessman once they got down to brass tacks. Probably surprised that she hadn't swooned at his charisma, but once the man got over himself, he had treated Kathra like any other businessman with whom deals could be made.

"I was amazed at how raw you decided to leave everything," Isaev continued, gesturing at the walls. Kathra's eyes followed his hands. "Most vessels I build spend substantial amounts of time and resources with insulation and paint to make things more…homey, I suppose."

"You've been aboard *WinterStar*," Kathra smiled starkly at the man. "Such things are unnecessary. We'll add a coat of paint here later, but I expect the crew to need to make modifications of the vessel over the next several years, once they get a feel for the habits they'll need."

She could see the confusion on the man's face, but he was used to building cargo vessels and yachts for rich playboys. People with money to burn.

Even after selling the rest of Daniel's collection, the Mbaysey wouldn't be rich. Just better off. Maybe enough to build a few more ships, recruit more crew, and go sailing.

And nobody outside the comitatus was aware that she planned to build a larger ship at some point. A CityStar that could hold as many as forty thousand people just on that one ship, with space to expand by adding more rings slowly over time as population grew.

It would not be a station, although it would act like one much of the time. More like a tiny Bishop ring with engines attached to a central hub, with enough surface area to include parks and orchards like Daniel had on his Turtle.

A place where the entire tribe could gather regularly, perhaps move to permanently, rather than having all the ClanStars, each with a tiny crew, isolated from one another most of the time and growing slowly into different cultures.

Over generations, that would be problematic, but Kathra was already planning for that day.

"It will be the work of my people to study every square centimeter of the surface," Kathra explained as the man's confusion remained present. "This is just a skeleton, that they will eventually turn into a home."

"And you still plan to return with more of those ships to sell?" he asked.

"Indeed, but I expect we'll auction some of those, just so your competitors have the chance to get involved and spend their own money on supporting my people."

"What else do you expect to find out there?" he asked, finally turning serious. "You wouldn't be dumping all of those ships now, unless there was something better to be had."

"I have my suspicions," Kathra replied with a conspiratorial smile that the man shared. "Daniel has his research and notes. But we won't know until we get there. At that point, we might be able to bring prizes back. At worst, I can hire a mobile dry-dock to haul something large or sell you the coordinates and let you retrieve it."

"Why?" he asked, suddenly turning cagey. "I've done my research and am frankly surprised that you were willing to deal at all with a male."

Kathra noted the way Isaev's majordomo cringed, and the comitatus warriors around the room bristled, ever so slightly. Nobody spoke, but eyes suddenly turned cruel and cold around her.

"I did my own research, Mikhail Isaev," she replied. "There are places I could have gone. Women I could have worked with, but your hatred of the Sept is something that tipped the scales in your favor."

"I do not hate the Sept Empire," he retorted.

"And you will barely trade with them at all, preferring to have all your corporate hulls go no farther than the last TradeStations in Free Worlds space," Kathra said.

"I wasn't aware that anybody was paying that close of attention," he blinked, somewhat surprised.

"What I was asking was a major undertaking, Factor Isaev," Kathra let her voice go almost as cold as the women around her. "And the Sept has made it clear that they would see the Mbaysey broken and returned to the Imperial fold. I will not allow it, but whoever I dealt with would come in for some level of Sept displeasure."

"And later, it will be worse?" he asked, licking his lips unconsciously.

Kathra shrugged, unwilling to speculate. The Sept might have left Azgon and decided to never bother her again.

And pigs might fly.

It would only be a matter of time. Or rather, distance. If they could not pursue her into uncharted, unclaimed space, they might have no choice but to grind their teeth and relinquish their revenge.

And pigs might fly.

"Who knows?" Kathra settled on. "Tavle Jocia is central on many trade routes, which is one of the reasons we picked it. It also provides a path for the Sept to strike here, as long we remain. Fortunately, they cannot send significant forces this deep into Free Worlds space, and SeekerStar can handle a Patrol."

"Should I look at building heavier vessels?" he asked.

Again, Kathra shrugged. If the Sept even threatened this system, she would probably never return to the Free Worlds. There were other TradeStations, further from Sept space, they just didn't have the ship-building capacity Mikhail Isaev had at his fingertips.

Perhaps she needed to just buy the sorts of oversized metal-stamping equipment that she could use to make a new ringship herself. *ForgeStar* already produced raw bar and sheet stock, most of which was used on the ships for repair and smaller tools.

She could be entirely free at that point, if she got desperate.

"Commander, I'm picking up an alarm from *WinterStar*," Ife called out. "Drives are beginning to charge for an unauthorized jump."

Kathra rounded on the Trade Factor, as though he was somehow at fault, but the man had gone pale, an ethnic risk with skin already nearly white to begin with. It wasn't him. But something had gone wrong with Erin and Daniel.

"Bring everything to alert and contact them immediately," Kathra ordered. "Get the Trade Factor to his shuttle in case we have to give chase. Someone stealing my ship won't ever be able to run far enough to escape me."

Stina stepped up and directed the two males off her bridge, while everyone else rocketed to the hallway and began to race outward to the launch tubes that would see their Spectres in space and ready to fight.

Kathra remained here. She would need to direct everything and SeekerStar had the firepower to destroy her old ship, if necessary. Hopefully, it wouldn't come to that.

THIRTY-ONE

DANIEL PULLED on the gloves to his suit as they traversed a long hallway with frequent warning signs that you were about to enter zones that might not be comfortable for humans. Technically, he wasn't sure he even qualified at this point, but his biology was still human, as were the four women with him.

He had never tried protecting four others with a defensive field, but maybe he could just cover their heads with breathable air if something bad happened. Maybe this was a dangerously stupid idea and he should just turn around right now and flee for his life.

It was a seductive idea. Just leave now and forget all this nonsense forever.

Daniel stopped and shook his head like he might rattle something loose. Around him, the four women had all come to a halt, almost like there was an invisible line in the deck, mocking them.

He growled when he realized that it really was an effect being projected on him. Something like he could do. Daniel and the others had just walked up to the outer edge of what he presumed was a zone of compulsion. A wall intended to drive him back quietly, and possibly without him even understanding why.

Anybody but a chef with a Golden Diamond awarded by Gastropode magazine, and it might have worked.

"What was that?" Erin snarled under her breath as she looked at him sideways.

"A figment of my imagination," Daniel snapped back at her. "We have arrived."

He started to take a step and realized that Iruoma was frozen in place. That surprised him, as he always thought of her as the fiercest of Kathra's warriors. Tattooing one's skull was one of the most painful places he could think of, and she had all manner of designs that she showed off daily by shaving her skull to a gleaming polish.

But there were whites visible around her dark pupils now. Her breathe was ragged and accelerated. Something about that barrier had gotten inside her mind, and it appeared to take everything she had right now just to stand still and not flee madly.

Daniel stepped in front of Iruoma and studied the woman. Dark brown skin clad in tangerine like a flame on a dark night.

Fierceness, incarnate.

"Iruoma?" he asked, but there was nobody home inside those eyes.

Terrified, but unwilling to admit it even to herself.

He grabbed her by the lapels and tugged until the woman looked down, staring into his face from ten centimeters away. Her eyes were like full moons at night now.

Daniel didn't want to test if his powers could work inside their field, since he had no idea what might happen if he did. Might warn them he was here.

Might even open him up for the sorts of domination by them that Urid-Varg had once done to these women, when that *salaud* had gotten into his mind the need for a harem.

He pulled her close and kissed her full on the lips, holding tight to her lapels as she suddenly struggled to pull away from him.

Surprise replaced fear on her face.

And then rage set in.

Daniel was pretty sure she was going to punch him now as he let go and she staggered backwards one step. He did deserve it, after all, but he'd been unable to think of another way to break through the fear that held her.

A fist came up and clenched in a rage so primal that he could smell it. This was going to hurt. But that was the price.

Instead of knocking his silly, *Rabic* ass onto the deck, though, Iruoma chuckled after a moment. She lowered her hand instead of punching him in the face.

"You could have just asked, Daniel," she said slyly.

"*Oui*," he agreed. "Maybe next time. For now, I figured that would get through anything those shits were doing to you. Areen is the only one that wouldn't want to kill me for taking such a liberty. And I'm sorry."

"Apology accepted," she said as her face cleared.

Before he could move, she grabbed him and returned the kiss. It wasn't passionate, but maybe more than the sort of thing she would give her sister. Maybe a really close sister, as some of them were.

He could be a sister to these women. There wasn't a higher compliment that he could think of.

"Are you two done?" Erin asked with a sour mom voice.

Daniel and Iruoma both turned and smiled at the boss.

He shrugged.

The seriousness on Erin's face deflated the balloon of

silliness that he had tried to wrap himself in. He nodded instead.

Serious business. Four women killers escorting him into the gates of whatever hell might await.

And whoever might be waiting beyond.

"WHAT IS OUR STATUS?" Pasdar asked as he again paced the length of the Great Causeway at the center of the ship's Command Node.

Aspbad Rostami walked over to one side to review the screens displayed below before answering, but Pasdar was not offended at the pause. Better to confirm your answer before speaking than to err at this critical junction.

"Squadron Command?" Rostami called to the man seated on the operations deck.

"Three Patrols are currently in place, awaiting orders, Aspbad," the man replied. "All ships have cleared for combat and charged their drives."

Pasdar nodded and stopped his pacing. He always found himself at the front of the node at moments like this, as though leading his men into battle, even though the Command Node itself was a tower rising above deck seventy almost at the center of the ship. At least a third of his men were closer to the enemy physically, but likely not emotionally.

Not today. Omezi was close out there. Distant

observations still showed her in orbit of Tavle Jocia, not far from the TradeStation where spies had placed her weeks ago.

Why she remained in the vicinity he did not know. Did not even particularly care, other than it made the chase that much easier for his fleet.

The Free Worlds would erupt in rage and complaint when a Septagon dropped out of jump this deep in their claimed space, but he was acting under orders of the Emperor himself. Further, he wouldn't be staying long. Patrol vessels had snuck close enough to the planet to note that the rest of Omezi's fleet had departed already, but *WinterStar* was still there.

It tantalized him, to think that they could surprise the woman and possibly destroy her and her flagship before she could react.

Pasdar knew he might never get an opportunity like this again.

"Aspbad?" he prompted Rostami, noting the hungry smile on the man's face as his mind went to similar places.

"Flight Operations, prepare for jump," Rostami called out, setting the table.

"Alert!" another man suddenly yelled. "Sensor readings have changed. Repeat sensor update. *WinterStar* has moved to trans-light and left the system. Another vessel appears to have left in pursuit."

Pasdar nearly snarled at the man, but those signals were already ten minutes old at this point, as far out as the squadron had landed to prepare for this last jump. *WinterStar* had already left, and Vorgash was only now catching up with that signal.

Still, if she wasn't here, he didn't have to provoke Tavle Jocia's authorities. Small victories in his wider campaign.

"Sensors, calculate her jump and triangulate," he ordered, skipping over Rostami, but it couldn't be helped.

Time was critical, if *WinterStar* had left. It would take precious minutes to identify where she had fled to, and then reprogram his own systems for the Patrols to give chase. Plus Vorgash was slower through jump, so Omezi would have extra time at the other end for mischief.

Maybe he would be lucky and she was leading him to her fleet, and he could round them all up at once.

The survivors, anyway.

Pasdar returned to his pacing. Any orders now would just delay his men. Rostami returned to his chair and sat patiently as well.

Several minutes passed like days as his Command crew consumed the signals and refactored everything.

"Naupati Pasdar, we have a course plotted," one of the man spoke up now. "Probability seventy-seven percent for their destination, based on nearby geography and gravitational geometry."

Pasdar walked over to look down on the man from the Causeway. He would have liked to actually lean over the man's shoulder to see the math itself, but he was three meters above him here, a downside of putting the commanders on their own mezzanine above.

Still, the screen before the man showed a course from Tavle Jocia that intercepted another star roughly fifteen light-years away. That one was marked uninhabited from the icons on the map, which made perfect sense. Omezi avoided others whenever possible, so she would have sent her forces to a quiet system for her rendezvous.

Someplace where Vorgash could drop out right on top of her, if the gods favored him, and he could destroy her. Better, perhaps he would be lucky enough to locate her alien allies and destroy them as well.

The Axial Megacannon was already charged for battle.

Fifteen light-years wouldn't take all that long that the charge would need to be bled off.

"Send the signal to the squadron," Pasdar ordered. "Vorgash will lead and all vessels conform their flight times to ours. We will transition to battle directly from jump so all vessels prepare in flight."

Pasdar paused to turn on his heel, taking in everything he could see from the large windows around him, as well as the men seated below.

He held the moment for a short stretch, knowing that signals would require a bit to reach everyone, even though they should have been prepared. If not, a Patrol vessel could move much faster than Vorgash, so they could catch up.

As long as everyone landed at once, he would be in a position to catch Omezi off-guard and finish her off for good.

"All vessels jump," he ordered.

THIRTY-THREE

NOW THAT HE knew what to listen for in his head, Daniel could see the lines of mental force that surrounded them constantly. He dared not seek out their source, because there seemed to be more than one of them, and they formed something of a net.

He would only get one chance at this sort of breaking and entering shenanigans. He needed to do it right.

This corridor wasn't like the other places on the station where he had roamed. The metal was heavier here. He couldn't think of a better way to describe it. It conveyed a solemnity of purpose that was much more brutal and unyielding than the other lobes.

Daniel interpreted that as being reinforced for all possible environments. Similarly, nothing was painted in the bright colors he had grown accustomed to. Everything was gray. Not steel gray, but a sealant primer designed to keep things from reacting.

He supposed that if you had to add trace elements to the air in places, you didn't want them reacting with the hull metal and weakening things, so he could understand that.

But it made him slightly miserable at some psychological level.

Plants. That was it. There were none, anywhere. In the human sections, there were always some around. The wealthier the deck, the more common the pots.

None of that was to be seen in any direction. Just metal walls and decks, painted with stripes in colors and patterns he presumed worked to direct someone to a particular destination, or at least an environment where one could relax and perhaps take off your breather mask.

They approached a lobby. That was the impression Daniel got of the volume as they entered the space. A three-deck-tall open space, such a tremendous waste of volume, but it lightened his mood, so perhaps that was why.

The ceiling was transparent as well, showing off the four towers around him and the stars straight up as he looked, so this was something of a courtyard, if you were on the surface of a planet instead of orbiting one.

"Now what?" Erin asked quietly.

They had the space to themselves, a circle roughly sixty meters across, broken up by tables, benches, and a few large planters that looked more to provide a modicum of visual privacy rather than for growing anything.

"You wait here," Daniel said.

He walked out into the middle of the space and found a compass rose that had been inset into the deck with gold-colored tiles. Each direction was marked, like they were on the surface of a planet again, and Daniel lined himself up with North.

Looking up, one of the four towers was directly in front of him, so he could see the purpose of the compass now. If you got lost, you came here and found the icons that matched up with where you were supposed to go.

Cheaper than having a human or other docent here to help travelers.

They were inside a zone of compulsion, but it was hollow. Just the suggestion at the edge, and then it fell off once you crossed an unseen line.

He did not go looking for the being generating the thing, so much as leaned back and stared at the tower, opening his mind to whatever it was. Daniel still lacked an adequate vocabulary to describe what he saw and how he did things, although Urid-Varg probably had had everything detailed.

Daniel could handle ignorance, if the alternative was going down that path.

Nothing stood out as he waited, so Daniel turned to the east and listened. The signal, whatever it was, was stronger here, but not much.

South lit his mind up when he turned. It almost felt like staring into the sun on a cloudy day. He checked west, just in case, but the signal tailed off, so whoever it was, whatever they were, was in the south tower.

Daniel narrowed his eyes, like he might narrow his mind, and began counting decks. They were much larger here than in the human sectors. Generally eight meters apart, presumably because some species might need sealed vehicles with their own environment, and chairs against the heavy gravity humans preferred.

Daniel knew of a few intelligent species that were primarily aquatic, so being in the air was like being in space to them. They drove around in portable swimming pools.

Eight decks up, the light was brightest. Or whatever it was. Daniel called it a mental spotlight. That was close enough, since he would need to share minds with someone else for them to even detect it, and he was pretty sure that would create a spotlight down here if he did.

Daniel came back to himself and felt a sweat break out,

as though someone had just turned the thermostat up. Kathra kept *WinterStar* warmer than any other ship Daniel had ever been aboard, but she didn't believe in heavy, wool clothing, either. Light and gauzy, whenever possible.

The air hadn't changed though. This was some new reaction to stress, he supposed.

A hand beckoned the warriors closer, moving on silent feet even when nobody was there to watch.

"Eighth deck, south tower," he murmured to Erin, suddenly feeling tired as well as overheated. "Let A'Alhakoth know."

Erin typed a quick message while Daniel concentrated on his breathing. After a moment, the strangeness passed and his core temperature fell back down to normal.

"Are you all right?" Iruoma whispered, stepping close to his side.

"If anyone else could do this, I'd let them," he told her honestly. "If any of you had sons you trusted, I would walk away from this thing in a heartbeat."

She nodded sympathetically, but there was nothing she could say. Some of the sons had stayed in the past, but the exceptionally strong-willed ones were normally left to find themselves a place in a galaxy where men dominated and they didn't have to be second-class citizens.

That might change in the future, if Kathra was successful at liberating the Mbaysey. If she built some of her dreams, there might be space for men as well, but the culture needed time to harden into a thing that would not lose its matriarchy quickly. Daniel was helping her buy that time.

After all, look at what the Sept had done, once they'd achieved power. And how hard Yagazie had had to fight to free the Mbaysey from their slavery, before freeing them from men entirely.

Daniel waited until Erin confirmed that the message had

been sent and then walked to the base of the south tower. A bank of elevators waited quietly, almost mocking him, but he didn't let that stop him from proceeding. He pushed a button and one of the doors opened immediately, welcoming him like a giant maw, all set to swallow the five of them.

He entered, and wondered if this was what hell felt like when you arrived.

THIRTY-FOUR

She felt like a princess in a fairy tale, going into the forest after a monster or a witch. A'Alhakoth paused to look at a reflection of herself in a window as she passed a storefront and shook her head at such silliness. Youngest of six children of the Count, with four older brothers and a sister ahead of her, so she wasn't remotely like a princess.

Her parents had not coddled her, either. She was as schooled and trained as her siblings, perhaps more so because she had always been daddy's special girl, and he wanted her to succeed on her own merits, rather than being sought as a political alliance of some sort.

She wasn't sure what marriage value she might bring, if and when she made it home to visit, but being an accepted warrior in a tribe of such women as the comitatus would certainly cause tongues to wag.

It would be even more interesting when Erin and the others would look all of her brothers in the eye, rather than letting the males lurk over them, like she had to.

The humans around her were like that as well, but they

couldn't generally help it. A'Alhakoth simply belonged to a species that was a head shorter, at least for the women. That wasn't about to stop her, though.

She stalked across the big mall space and exited the nominally-human areas for the sections of the TradeStation where the aliens lived. The other aliens. She could pass as human. Could be mistaken for one if the lighting wasn't good or she had a hood of some sort she could pull up, like the girl in the fable.

The locals in this lobe of the station would treat her like a human if she encountered one, whatever that meant.

She moved into hallways that were only sparsely inhabited, until she was alone as far as she could see in either direction. At least to the hatches at each end of the walkway.

Good enough. A'Alhakoth pulled out her skyvox and tuned it to listen. No signal from Erin, and the woman's own skyvox was far enough away that A'Alhakoth couldn't get a signal to triangulate on.

Her job wasn't to stay close to the others, but rather to get just to the edge of such range and track them. It was up to her to make sure nobody snuck up on them while they were working, or for her to come in and surprise someone who had surprised them.

A beep let her know she had a message.

South tower, eighth floor.

Erin was probably two hallways ahead of her, already at the base of the tower quad, and Daniel had found something. A'Alhakoth still didn't understand how any of that worked, other than the gem seemed to be the genesis of it. Humans didn't have such powers, although she had encountered a few rumors of species that did.

Was Daniel human anymore? He was alien to her, but human and kaniea weren't all that different physically. All of her brothers and her father were taller and heavier than the cook, but she'd be willing to give the small human male even odds, even without the aid of that gem.

She'd seen the inside of his mind, just as he had seen hers. If one could somehow bottle the distilled stubbornness that seemed to be Daniel's soul and sell it as a magical potion, A'Alhakoth imagined she might get rich.

She pressed on, keeping the skyvox in one hand but down at her side. Her eyes sought every nook and hallway, as though an assassin might be lurking. Kanus wasn't so advanced as a culture that people never resorted to simple violence to make a point.

But she was alone.

A'Alhakoth wondered if this section was just overbuilt against future need, or if there weren't that many truly alien creatures aboard right now that they needed such quarters. She was just fine in the human sections, as long as she watched her back. Similarly, Vida or Se'uh'pal could make do over there without much work.

It would make it much easier, if Daniel didn't have to wade through the entirety of the alien sections of the haystack to find the needle he wanted.

She found the quad at the base of the tower. The navigational cross was still there, from where she'd visited when she'd first come aboard, before it became obvious how much cheaper it was to live as a poor human, rather than an alien with any sort of special needs.

A'Alhakoth found a spot mostly out of sight of the south tower elevators and studied her skyvox. Erin was just at the edge of her range now, flickering in and out of signal, since it didn't necessarily have to punch through many decks if she was beneath the stars.

This would be a good place to watch. And wait.

Anyone approaching from the human sections wouldn't necessarily see her, and if they did, she was blue, rather than pink or brown, so they wouldn't immediately associate her with the Mbaysey. In that, Commander Omezi had chosen well.

THIRTY-FIVE

THE LIFT DOORS OPENED SILENTLY. Daniel stared out into an enormous space, feeling like a child. The doors themselves were five meters wide, across the whole facing of the lift. The ceiling in here was four meters, but out there it was closer to seven.

Seriously, he was six years old again and walking into one of those tremendous cathedrals that the colonists seemed to build third on every planet they hit, right after the first bar and the first restaurant.

Everywhere, the scale was intimidating.

Or was it? He turned to the four warriors with him and each of them had that same look of awe on her face.

Damn it, you salauds. *I'm running out of patience with your mind games.*

He grabbed Erin by the hand and pulled her to face him.

"This is all an illusion," he said in a taut growl.

She blinked, and then growled back at him as the light came on in her eyes.

Daniel nodded and looked, but the others had broken the grip of whatever it was when he spoke. *They* had set it up to make you feel tiny and vulnerable when you stepped out onto this deck. The scale of construction was purposeful, but that was the mechanics of dealing with alien needs.

Someone was reinforcing the feeling of inferiority. They had chosen the wrong cast of women to use it on. Kam started to draw her pistol, but Erin barked at her and it went back into the holster.

For now.

Daniel stepped out onto the deck of the eighth floor and moved forward some for the others to clear the lift. Steel floors and walls. Lights an impossible distance away overhead, at least to someone used to the much-smaller decks of a human starship.

Three hallways led from here, down the two sides and right into the middle of the tower building itself. He pivoted in place, letting the music in his mind draw him. This tower was round, rather than square, so the two side hallways eventually connected on the far edge, he supposed, and the one in the middle was a spoke to a central hub he could see some distance down the way. It let him divide things slowly into halves.

There. Maybe. That light was brighter on the left as he faced the center of the tower.

Daniel started walking slowly down the spoke, keeping his mind as compact as he could against what felt like a mental wind blowing in his face. None of the women seemed to be feeling anything like it, so perhaps it was just him.

Just him and whoever they were.

He felt Kam standing on his right, back a meter where she could draw and fire if she needed to. Similarly, Nkechi was on his left, and closer, so she could rush up and grapple a foe that stepped out.

Hopefully, it wouldn't come to that, because Daniel didn't think that the women would be able to resist. He considered sending them home right now, but couldn't be sure if those were his thoughts, concerned for their safety, or someone else worried that these women were more dangerous than the strangers could handle.

In for a pfennig, in for a drachma. All of them were volunteers, and warriors.

The whole point of Kathra's comitatus was a set of women willing to die for her. And one Algerian chef who would die with them if it came to that.

THIRTY-SIX

Erin took up a spot at the rear of their little convoy, so that she could keep an eye on the others. She figured that those three were so keyed up right now that stopping them from doing extravagant violence was more likely than spurring them.

She walked quietly. People never really gave her credit for how carefully she could set her metal foot down on the deck when she wanted to. Today, she had almost gone peg leg under her pants. Just the rubberized heel for gripping, but not the toe section that made it look like a normal foot.

If she had to kick someone, they were getting raw metal without any padding. Erin figured that they'd be deserving it at that point.

She had her skyvox down at one side, on but not transmitting anything more than a location signal for the station. And A'Alhakoth.

Erin had programmed an emergency button on it and had her thumb close enough to hit it if something went wrong, so both A'Alhakoth and Kathra would be alerted.

What they might do in that situation was iffy, but Erin

had gotten that stupid macho crap pounded out of her a long time ago. She had twenty sisters she could call on if she needed them.

And a pair of warships.

Daniel led them like a bloodhound on a short leash, his head turning back and forth like he was sniffing a trail. In a way, he was.

Kam and Nkechi stayed close, which was why she'd picked them. Others might be better pilots, or smarter warriors, but those two were the best at their chosen form of violence, which said a lot in the comitatus.

Iruoma was here because Daniel had asked. And Erin didn't mind. That scowl she habitually wore was intense enough to maybe curdle milk today, if they ran into any.

She had no idea what they would find here. Not even theories, because any guess she planned on would likely be wrong and color all her decisions and mistakes that much more.

Urid-Varg had been on the move for nearly a thousand years at the point he died, according to stories Daniel had shared. Not in a direct line for human space, but more like a random zig-zag across space. It was as if he would stay in one place for a while, and then move on when his current host body got old. Sometimes he would take another of the same kind, but more frequently he must had heard tales of a more interesting species nearby.

Twelve thousand years was a short time, as far as planets and species went, but the galaxy had also come alive with new travelers, as one species might encounter a few neighbors and provide them with space travel, either by conquering them as a pocket empire, or via trade.

Empires never really lasted long in space. Travel times between stars meant communication was slow. Humans were ascendant right now only because the Sept Empire was vigorously enforcing a specism of human supremacy, but even then, you had to face the tightly-bound rules and laws of caste that put Persian men at the top of the pyramid and slowly worked down to African women. Only the aliens were more despised.

The Sept would fail. The Mbaysey were just the first step in all the pieces that would spall off and leave for a better life elsewhere. Eventually, enough renegade humans would join up with enough pissy aliens, and the Sept would be squashed.

Daniel's Turtle might even help, although Erin had her doubts that something like that would happen in her lifetime. And nobody had any idea how long Daniel might live.

Daniel reached the center of the tower. He walked into the middle of a kind of greathall, maybe fifteen meters across and round, while Erin stayed clear out on the edge. They had ignored two more hallway rings leading to apartments getting here, and found themselves in a lounge, Erin supposed.

A space where you might entertain someone close to your suite, if maybe it wasn't safe for them to enter? Gravity too high? Maybe a weird atmosphere that most folks couldn't breathe?

She had no idea. Until the tribe had permanently left Sept space, their encounters with aliens were extremely rare, and mostly Vida or Se'uh'pal, the explorers and merchants of space, respectively. At least according to their own legends. Even Vida were rare.

Se'uh'pal were almost like fleas on the back of a dog, the little rabbit-like bipeds unafraid to go anywhere and trade for anything.

But they didn't need special environments, either of them. Who the hell would hide here?

Unless they wanted you to think they were completely alien.

Erin grinned at a sudden, mischievous thought. Take rooms in the alien section, and tell people you were a mesomorph, a literal shapechanger, and watch their eyes get big.

It was an evil idea. She made a note to talk to Kathra about pulling such a prank on some TradeStation, sometime in the future. Presumably one they were only visiting once in passing and never coming back.

She watched Daniel rotate in place once more, like a searchlight or a lighthouse maybe. He paused at a certain spot then continued, coming back to that spot.

"There," he muttered. "Second ring, if I have triangulated them correctly. *Certainement*, we shall discover the truth soon enough."

Erin nodded to the women and moved past the entryway where she had waited as Daniel picked the closest of the six hallways and moved.

All of these corridors were oversized. Moving heavy equipment, Erin supposed. Or bizarre mobile life support systems if you were alien enough to need them, but still capable of communicating with humans and the like.

Daniel paused at the first intersection and looked all directions, like a feral dog wanting to cross a busy street. Or a bloodhound on the scent.

He turned left and moved into the ring. Erin let some space open up, but not enough that she lost sight of the others. She noted a doorway and thought about sending A'Alhakoth a message, but feared that the aliens might hear it somehow and know that they were being pursued.

The walls were still rough metal painted gray, with nothing in the way of decorations. The air tickled her nose.

Just enough ammonia to detect, but not enough to make her sneeze.

Her chef found the hatch he wanted. She watched him stop and pivot to his right, staring so intently she wondered if he could somehow see through the steel.

He turned to her and she could see a cold fire in those eyes.

Daniel nodded to her but didn't speak, as though he was afraid to rouse the ghosts. The three women turned to her for instructions and she nodded back, gesturing for them to spread out.

As before, Nkechi was close and Kam back a little. Erin took a spot to one side and back, with Iruoma mirroring her. Daniel stood at the hatch itself, and seemed to be only partly present.

Gone away inside his mind, perhaps.

He glanced back both directions to confirm his helpers, and pressed the door lock.

Erin wondered if that would sound a bell and bring the aliens to the door, like a pizza delivery, but the hatch opened.

A smell escaped the room, but she couldn't place it. Not toxic. Organic and slightly musky. Not entirely unpleasant, but weird.

Daniel entered. Nkechi and Kam went next. Erin nodded Iruoma in and waited at the door.

Inside, another waiting room, completely bare of furniture, but with generic watercolor prints framed and hanging on three walls, with doors leading off on all sides.

They were committed now. Erin stepped into the room and let the hatch close behind her. It was a standard door, so her pistol could do enough damage that she could pry it open, before she had to reload. Plus she had the other three women.

Daniel moved to the door on the inner wall. It wasn't

even as heavy as the one to the suite. Painted steel, but the kind that rested on a roller track with a magnetic slider mechanism to move it.

The smell was stronger in here. Erin decided that must be what the aliens smelled like when they hadn't had a bath in a while. She followed Daniel to the door and watched him open it.

The room beyond was dim enough that she could make out shapes when she followed the others in, but not much detail.

Couches, maybe. Bookcases on a few walls. Carpeting on the floor that was just thick enough to provide her foot a little better traction than the steel, but not much more.

Anything more she wanted to think or do ceased as a hand came down and grabbed hold of her mind, squeezing painfully and severing all contact with her hands, feet, or mouth.

The lights came up suddenly and Erin saw movement.

THIRTY-SEVEN

He held his breath as he opened the outer hatch, but nothing jumped out at them. Daniel had been sure that it was all a trap, but simply could not determine if the best choice was to flee or to confront it.

He didn't think he could live the rest of his life with whatever it was lurking over him. Best to face it now.

The room had a familiar feeling to it, but nothing he could identify. Just bare walls with the pictures that the station had hung, but it almost felt like coming home.

Weird.

The four women were still with him, but they were better warriors than he was. All of them.

Any of them.

At least that would drive his male ego into not surrendering.

The siren call was coming from ahead of him, deeper into the suite. He moved to the door he wanted and pressed the button to slide it into the wall.

Darkness beyond. Well, dimness. The sort of shadows you got with the lights on the second-lowest setting, just enough to navigate a dark bedroom on the way to pee, if you woke up in the middle of the night.

The outer room had been bare, but this space was crowded. Almost messy. Lumps and shapes Daniel felt like he should be able to identify, but the words were only at the tip of his tongue and slid away before he could taste them.

At least the smell was right. He was back in his kitchen on Genarde, about to pull the perfect apple pie from the stove and rest it in the pie safe to perfume the entire restaurant with fall goodness.

Except there were no apples here. And Genarde was a thousand light-years away.

Daniel started to turn to say something to Erin. To alert her that something was wrong with his perceptions, his whole world.

The first attack hit his mind like a wet towel slung by a rude cook as he stepped to the door of his office to look out at the noise. He was blind and surprised.

No pain, but shock.

Daniel staggered back mentally and suddenly he was cut off from the four women who had come with him to their dooms. Their presence had lifted him at those moments when despair wanted to take root and drive him back to his bed.

Never.

The lights came up now as he fought back.

Faces rose from the couches around him and focused their will, their rage upon him.

Daniel managed to hold his barriers, but he had only perhaps a centimeter beyond his skin, and their mental blows rang on his shields like hammers beating a sword into shape.

He could see what they were now.

Unbidden, a word finally made it as far as his mouth, but

he had clenched his jaws when the blow hit, so he could not say it aloud.

Ishtan.

In person, they looked like giant snakes covered over in a pink-ish fur almost as long as one of his fingers. Bodies six to ten meters long and almost as big as his narrow chest. Two arms near the top of the body for manipulating dexterously, with four fingers counter-opposed by two thumbs.

The jaw would split into three, equal parts, revealing three, bright-blue tongues. In each jaw was an eye, a multi-faceted orb that reminded Daniel of a fly, magnified a thousand time in a microscope.

There were six of them, a perfect hunting party. He didn't know how he knew that, but the knowledge was there in the back of his mind as he fought them.

His four friends would be no help. Dimly, he sensed that one of the ishtan had simply taken control of them, rendering them immobile while the other five pressed hard against his shields and tried to reach inside his mind.

It would be like Urid-Varg had returned, except this time he wouldn't be missed in the creature's arrogant assumption that Kathra Omezi, the great warrior Commander with her all-female comitatus, would never have a male serving her.

These creatures had come for him. Perhaps they had been stalking Urid-Varg for all this time, and that was what had driven the monster into human space.

You are correct, Daniel Lémieux, one of them pulsed at him. *Your time is ended. Your evil will not stand.*

Behind him, Daniel heard the sounds of four women crashing bonelessly to the deck, and then the weight of a sixth mind suddenly landed upon his shoulders.

He growled in rage as the weight became unbearable. There was no thought of attacking, as the six of them thrust bolt after mental bolt at him and it was all he could do to deflect them and hold.

Slowly, they pushed him back into himself. Daniel felt like he was trying to hold up *WinterStar* by himself, standing on some ice planet in tunnels hollowed out by pink, furry bodies.

"I am not him!" Daniel screamed at the creatures, but it made no difference.

Six minds pressed down on him until they were inside his own mind now. Daniel resisted, but felt himself giving way under the assault, like the worst migraine he had ever had described to him, with someone having filled his veins with mercury and then applied a current that outlined every blood vessel in his skull so brightly that even he was blinded.

Finally, Daniel lost control of his flesh, having retreated to a small ball of impotent fury at the very center of his being.

He watched as if from outside himself as the body of Daniel Lémieux stepped awkwardly forward and sat on a chair, a human implement completely at odds with the rest of the furnishings in here.

Two of the ishtan slithered forward and bound his hands and ankles to the chair with strange hands that ended in four claw-tipped fingers opposed by two thumbs. They relaxed their stranglehold on his body at that point, but remained fiercely evident in his upper mind, like six strangers standing on an iced-over pond while he swam below.

At least he was not drowning, but there was precious little he could do but watch as they plundered his memories, seeking something.

Almost negligently, one of them turned to the four women. One by one, they rose, like awkward zombies or badly-programmed robots, staggering forward to sit next to each other on one of the couches.

Six ishtan surrounded him, even though he could only see three, with hints of two others weaving like mesmerized snakes on his peripheral vision.

Where is the xxxxxxxxx? one of them pounded on the ice with a mental bellow.

"The what?" he couldn't help but reply, confused.

An image appeared on the ice. Or whatever the barrier was that they had erected, once they had driven him back far enough to plunder his mind.

The Star Turtle.

"Why?" he demanded of them.

Your evil will not stand, the strongest of them screamed back.

Daniel didn't have an answer to that. Much of what he could do could only be described as evil. Even he said that.

But he had never met anyone else that would be a better choice, since the power was utterly gendered and no female could wield it.

Of course not, somebody said.

"Of course what?" Daniel channeled his fury to the surface.

No female should have power, one of the ishtan snarled in that mental space they occupied. *They were egg-layers. Not intelligent creatures.*

"Fools," Daniel felt heat finally ignite in his bones. It gave him the strength to drive himself to the surface and confront them again. "In my world, they can be queens."

His rage caught them by surprise. That much was obvious.

Where before he had been held under ice but not drowning, now Daniel found himself falling into one of their minds instead.

THIRTY-EIGHT

HEAT.

That was the impression Daniel had as his mind opened inside the other being, like a flower discovering morning dew.

The ishtan were from a cold planet. This room had the heat turned down considerably, but it was still too warm for the being to be comfortable.

Daniel had been inside other minds before this. Those could not resist him, but the ishtan were different. They could fight.

He had surprised this one with his rage and managed to penetrate the being's mental barriers.

It would not be for long. Already, he could feel the male ishtan (they were all male?) begin to recoil from assaulting Daniel and preparing to thrust the intruding alien back out of his own head. Daniel leapt down into the creature's memories as hard as he could, absorbing everything he could reach without bothering to sort it.

Anything to understand how they came to be here, and why they were so intent on Daniel and the Turtle.

He felt like a five-year-old with money from grandpa again, setting foot into the candy store where everything was a wondrous joy to behold, and he didn't know where to start.

Daniel opened his mouth and sucked memories in like one of the great whales on Earth, moving on from recent to the deepest ones he could find.

Who were the ishtan? What was their connection to Urid-Varg? Why were they here? Why did they need a Star Turtle?

He held them off as long as he could, but eventually five of them managed to grab enough of Daniel's mind to drag him kicking and screaming out into the air and push him back into his own body.

Six faces close enough now to smell him, except that the ishtan had almost no olfactory senses, given the warrens of tunnels under stone and ice where they had developed.

Daniel felt the heat of a shallow volcano warm a breed of creatures midway between lizard and snake, still retaining the forelimbs, even as they evolved their latter legs away in favor of slithering and tunneling, deep down where they only emerged to hunt and scavenge.

Males had developed the mental powers of the gem to aid in hunting silently, but for whatever reason, the females were barely intelligent enough to have language.

Daniel had impressions of ice fields warmed from below, just enough heat and life that groups of ishtan could evolve intelligence and tool usage. Memories of monsters on the surface seeking prey and willing to risk ice worm tunnels, until those turned into hunting traps. Similarly, strange, six-legged creatures that reminded Daniel of terriers, charging into the tunnels to bite and rend, until they were somehow domesticated into the same tribal role that wolves had taken, once they turned into dogs.

So, this was their home.

It was, human, a voice answered, surprising him even more than the assaults had done. *It is no more.*

Daniel felt the one whose memory he had looted turn to him now and focus. They had both rifled each other's past. It would come to know him almost as well as he did it, given time.

That was before the Destroyer came, the male continued.

Daniel had an image of a creature invading the tunnels. A biped, wearing a familiar-enough-looking bodysuit, lime green with white stripes as wide as Daniel's hand connecting to white gloves and boots just like he wore, and the white belt invisible under Daniel's outfit.

It was still there.

The only difference was the lack of that platinum housing embedded directly into the creature's breastbone, just below the neck.

Rather than mental powers, the creature used technology. A weapon that was a close- equivalent to a modern beam rifle reached out and slaughtered ishtan as they first stood and later fled. A device on the creature's belt emitted a painful field that made thought impossible and communication difficult, rendering the ishtan even more vulnerable, just another species standing alone against an alien invader.

A memory from Urid-Varg's deepest layers bubbled up inside Daniel now.

He had built a device that would jam the mental abilities of the native species in his quest for power. It somehow screamed across a number of frequencies that they used, allowing him to defeat their greatest ability and leaving them nothing more than garden snakes.

The ishtan used tools, but were not a warlike species, like humans or Urid-Varg's people. They fell before him one by one, until the destroyer found the creature he sought.

Daniel felt his breath catch at the image. Each of these

specimens around him were between six and eight meters long, but the one Urid-Varg found and killed was a monster so much larger that it almost defied belief, perhaps nearly thirty meters. Enormous. Ancient.

Powerful beyond all others of their kind.

He watched Urid-Varg kill the ancient one with his beam weapon, and then chop his front fifth off and carry it away on a sled that floated on magnetic fields.

Because the others had rifled his own mind, Daniel's memories of Urid-Varg were stirred up and near the surface. Perhaps they were driving him to remember things he didn't even understand to look for.

Urid-Varg returned to a starship on the surface of the world, parked on a rocky outcropping against the risk of ice collapsing under the weight. Daniel did not recognize the ship, but it was not much larger than the four craft he had given Kathra to sell to the Trade Factor. Perhaps a yacht, except it was armed.

Urid-Varg retreated aboard his craft and lifted off, carrying his prize to orbit, where he took his tools and separated the ancient one's skull into six pieces down the suture lines. Blue tongues. Blue blood. Pink fur.

Daniel watched himself reach into the gory mass inside the creature's brain and pull something out, like a fisherman opening an oyster for a pearl. Urid-Varg washed the stone, tested it with some esoteric machine, and began laughing maniacally.

Daniel remembered walking to the front of his ship with the ancient one's mind gem clenched in one fist, still laughing. Sitting in the command chair and targeting the planet below.

A strike of anti-matter bombs blasted the surface of the world like a giant asteroid impacting. Debris was thrown as high as the orbit where Urid-Varg could fly through them, listening to the patter of dust and glass sphericals bouncing off his hull.

Daniel opened Urid-Varg's hand and recognized the gem. It was attached to his bodysuit right now, under his shirt.

Urid-Varg had killed most of the ishtan, after taking the mind gem from the ancient one to use as a weapon. After becoming a conqueror.

All of the ishtan, the voice corrected Daniel. *There are no more egg-layers.*

"You are immortal?" he gasped.

Close enough, the voice said. *We have pledged to hunt the Destroyer and end his evil. That time is at hand.*

"I am not him," Daniel cried, but it was like trying to break down a brick wall with his breath, and he was no wolf.

His power must be destroyed.

Something like a mental fist came up and ended the conversation by punching him in the brain.

PART THREE
ISHTAN

THIRTY-NINE

SHE WAITED with all the patience of a sixth child and second daughter, always last in line and told not to fidget as she waited her turn. A'Alhakoth paid attention to the noise around her, but there was no traffic in or out of this section of the station right now.

She wondered if the battle she expected to be playing out above her had driven all the casual witnesses off, like a sudden, heavy rain grounding wet and frustrated birds until it passed.

Erin had not moved for several minutes, according to the screen A'Alhakoth watched now. She was right at the edge of range, but the lack of overhead decks helped the signal, so it was mostly strong enough to be clear.

Ah, spoke to soon.

She watched Erin's signal moving now. Retracing her steps presumably back to the lift in order to return to the main parts of the station. Except that there should be some signal, some message that indicated a change of plans or a failure to find that which they sought.

A'Alhakoth considered the powers that the human male

Daniel manifested, and who might be able to hide from him. Had someone ambushed Erin and the other women and taken them?

Was it possible to ambush such people in reverse and liberate her new comrades? Daniel struck with the speed of thought. She would have perhaps a half second in which to act, before someone like him could capture her the same way.

Movement suggested other outcomes. That her friends were now prisoners, and headed somewhere, although A'Alhakoth could not, for the life of her, imagine where they might go. There was no place on the station any better, if you had prisoners such as these and wished to do something with them.

That suggested that they were leaving.

Did they have a ship parked somewhere? That made the most sense. Having captured Daniel and the comitatus warriors, whoever it was might want to leave the station to do whatever evil they had in mind.

She rose from her bench and made her way to the corridor out. Back to the human sections of the station.

Erin had parked her *SkyCamel* in the usual dock. It was unarmed, but equipped now with a valence drive. A'Alhakoth had no idea if SeekerStar was ready for deep space flight yet, and *WinterStar* was in the process of being emptied of all but a skeleton crew so it could be flown to a resting place and shut down for now.

At least until Kathra Omezi's Mbaysey were large enough to need it. Hopefully, A'Alhakoth would have qualified to fly a Spectre by then, and could join the warriors protecting the entire tribe. She felt like a precocious child graduating early and setting out on some quest.

Again.

Erin's signal was in the lift now, descending in such a way that the signal itself began to degrade. Too much steel in the way, especially as A'Alhakoth began to jog to the SkyCamel. She needed to be there and have completed her pre-flight before Erin and the others got wherever they were going. Plus, she could contact the Commander and let her know that something had gone wrong, so she could prepare to intercept whatever ship the aliens were using.

Briefly, she wondered if Daniel's powers could protect the four women, if Kathra Omezi were to destroy the ship they were in and dump them into vacuum. That would hamper any rescue efforts.

It might come down to the newest warrior in the tribe. She gulped and began to jog, weaving her way in between pedestrians on the main concourse.

Time might be running out for everyone.

Faster than she expected, A'Alhakoth got to the SkyCamel and cycled herself aboard. She raced to the cockpit and pulled out the pre-flight checklist, handily kept on a clipboard nearby for someone still learning how to fly the class in order to remember everything.

A SkyCamel was a long box with engines on the sides. A cockpit with two seats, where Erin always flew and Daniel always rode next to her. Storage closet and privy just behind that, through an interior hatch, and then the cargo bay itself, stripped down to almost bare walls and lined with jumpseats a woman could pull down and strap herself into. Aft, there was a small engineering bay on one side, for accessing fuel tanks and various things, and an airlock on the left, as she faced rear.

This particular vessel had been used as a runabout between the two big ships, when Erin needed to be going back and forth with supplies and orders. As a result, there were a couple of boxes back there, both roughly the size of double-tall coffins, where random things could be stashed so they didn't move around when the vessel was in zero-g.

A'Alhakoth moved down her checklist, keeping an eye on her skyvox and turning on her local scanners to track traffic around the station. She also brought up the main station control channel on her screen, watching for departures to suddenly be added, so she would know which vessel to follow.

Just as she reached for the vox, in order to brief the Commander on the situation, the outer lock on her SkyCamel began to cycle, beeping to let everyone know that the heavy door was in the process of moving, so they could get out of the way.

She had gotten so wrapped up in pre-flight that she'd forgotten her skyvox. It showed Erin standing just outside on the concourse.

They were about to leave in this ship?

She was trapped. The door would open in about fifteen seconds and she would have to risk a gunfight, right here in the SkyCamel.

Or would she?

A'Alhakoth unbuckled from the pilot's seat and moved aft. There was the privy and the storage closet. Neither sounded appealing, as hijackers with any sense would poke a nose into both, just to make sure they were alone.

She would have.

That left the two coffins aft. And hardly any time to reconsider her insanity as she raced to the aft one, popped the locks holding it closed, and threw herself in.

Hopefully, nobody would notice that someone had left the lid unlocked and do something about it. She found a crossbar inside, grabbed it, and pulled the lid back down on the hinges, plunging herself into total darkness.

At least the box wasn't airtight, as pressure differentials were common between ships and stations, and you didn't want anything exploding suddenly.

At the same time, she was in a gray box in total darkness, when her mind wanted to interpret everything as being in a coffin, where she was about to be lowered into the ground and buried alive.

At least it wasn't spiders. This was a nightmare she felt she could contain. Spiders would have her out of the box, screaming and firing.

Outside, as she tried to calm her breathing, the inner lock beeped. On her skyvox, she could see Erin enter the vessel and move directly to the pilot's seat.

She could hear other noises. Perhaps jumpseats being lowered and used.

There was absolutely no conversation.

Other than training, A'Alhakoth couldn't remember a time when those women weren't cracking jokes or talking about some fantastic meal Daniel had prepared for them. A'Alhakoth had always been closer to her closest brothers, Kilra and Trelga, rather than her sister E'Elbarth, so she had recognized the banter when they admitted her to the comitatus.

Utter silence baffled her.

Unless they had all somehow been *taken*. There was that.

A sound directly above her caused A'Alhakoth's hand to slip into her jacket for a pistol she had not brought with her before she remembered where she was.

Fists and clubs. The Commander had wanted prisoners.

The sound above had been a body sliding onto the top of her box, as though whoever it was would fly without a jumpseat to hold them when the SkyCamel escaped the grav field inducers of the station. That was even more insane than total silence.

But if they were taking this SkyCamel, it would make it easier for her to follow.

If only she had been smart enough to call the

Commander first, but she'd been wrapped up in her own fantasies of riding to the rescue. She had forgotten the first rule of the comitatus: *We are legion*.

There was nothing A'Alhakoth could do now but ride helplessly along, and hope that she could fix her error before it was too late.

FORTY

THERE WAS a rage in her soul so deep and so grand that Erin was surprised she didn't just erupt in flames, like the evil djinn from the story.

Not that she could do anything.

Daniel talked about the left hand of evil. Of all the terrible things a person with mental powers such as his could do to a woman, once she was in his control. But Daniel was a male. He thought about the physicality of rape.

The act of forcing a woman to have sex, even to enjoy it. As if that was all that rape consisted of.

Foolish male had no idea. But his heart was in the right place. She had continued to verify that on a regular basis, every time he opened his mind to her.

Erinkansilemi Uduik would know the man was turning evil before he did. She would feel a few moments of regret when it became necessary to kill him, but as he said, such power corrupted even the most innocent souls.

These furry fuckers were going down in the hardest, nastiest way she and all her sisters could come up with.

Rape was a physical act. It didn't happen in the tribal

squadron, on penalty of a slow, painful death, but there were women alive, elders who remembered the days when the women of the Mbaysey were *property*.

Grandma Ezinne still bore the barcode tattoo on her cheek, just as Erin did.

Rape was a crime of power, not sex.

A person could take, because nobody could stop them. Daniel had that potential in him, but he worked hard every day to keep it as far away from himself as possible, lest he become the thing he hated most in the universe.

These pink snakes just took.

Erin fought, but there was precious little she could do. The others were certainly struggling just as hard, but they lacked the raw power necessary to change things. At least the four of them required the attention of one of the snakes, lest they break out. The other five were too much for Daniel to overcome, but someone would have a lapse.

It was human nature, and Erin was willing to bet that it was snake nature, too. Even pink, furry monsters like these.

She felt scaly hands rifling through her mind. They dug into the older memories, but really only seemed interested in Urid-Varg.

Erin found herself reliving the day she first met that *salaud*. Awakening from a daze to find herself naked in the flight bay, with Kathra and Iruoma also stripped.

And Daniel standing over the body of Urid-Varg, the little fucker's head staved in by a fire suppressor. A heavy, steel one.

Later, trying to determine what the being was. And stopping Daniel when he fell prey to some last trap Urid-Varg had left behind.

Kathra killing the creature.

Daniel almost becoming him.

Eyes looked around now. Erin had the impression of someone sniffing, but the scent they wanted wasn't here.

The largest snake had taken up station aft after he had forced Erin into the pilot's seat, like was normal. Daniel rode next to her, just as glassy-eyed as the rest.

Ndidi, the voice called.

Erin shrugged, at least as much as her mind was allowed.

All eyes turned to Daniel now. Erin heard him make a strangled, almost choking sound as her own hands began the pre-flight checklist. It went quickly, but it always did. She didn't leave things for later, if they needed doing now.

If there was a hand on the top of her head, pushing her mohawk down, it shifted now. Daniel was resisting them, and it took the efforts of all six to pry open his mind.

Their intense hold never wavered, but she could hear snippets of conversation, as if the aliens were talking, but need to focus all their will on Daniel to keep him from erupting.

Erin was made of fire, but these snakes did not feel her heat.

WinterStar, one of them whispered.

A memory had been pried from her mind, showing just how empty her old home was, with nearly everyone on SeekerStar now. There was just enough of a skeleton crew to fly the ship.

Another image, showing the Star Turtle in orbit where they had left it before coming to this TradeStation. Minds read the stars in the background.

Erin found herself manipulating controls to bring everything live and separate from the station. She was laying in a course to *WinterStar*, presumably to dock.

She assumed that the snakes were going to hijack the ship, from the whispers she overheard. Nobody had mentioned to them that a SkyCamel also had a tiny valence drive. Slow and relatively short-ranged, but flying to the Turtle was possible, although the life support might be strained by the time they got there.

Erin focused her mind on *WinterStar*, lest they somehow realize their mistake. That ship moving would get Kathra's attention, and Ife would come after them. Howling like all the demons of hell.

Hopefully, that many angry minds would be too much for the snakes to control, and someone could break loose long enough do something nasty. Once Daniel was free, things were going to get ugly.

Once she was free, there would be blood.

"*WinterStar*, this is Erin in SkyCamel Six, departing the station," she found herself saying. "Got a package to drop off on my way to SeekerStar."

"Acknowledged, SkyCamel Six," came the reply. "Your usual spot is currently available."

Deep inside, Erin felt a chuckle, but it withered in the heat. All spots were currently available on the old flagship.

Erin's hands undocked from the station and applied just enough power to begin the transition. Grav Field Inducers let go quickly, and everyone was in freefall. There were no squawks, so she presumed that the snakes had hooked their tails onto something as they floated.

The humans had all been buckled in tight.

"Erin, this is Kathra," the Commander came over the line. "Status?"

She felt hands rifle through her mind, looking for the trap contained in that conversation.

"Mission mostly successful," she replied against her will, even sounding breezy and cool as she did. "Will explain everything when we get to SeekerStar."

As in, I'm fine. The crew is fine. Nobody has a gun to our

heads, and this is an open line, so I don't want to let anyone else out there listening know our secrets.

Damn it. None of her mind was hers.

They could open her up like a book, find the page they needed, and read the words aloud with her mouth.

Kathra would not suspect anything, but would be patiently waiting while Erin intercepted *WinterStar* and dropped off whatever it was she was carrying. And then the older ship would jump straight to where the Star Turtle was and these *salauds* would be free to do whatever it was they had in those furry minds.

She had failed.

Damn it.

FORTY-ONE

Instead of jumping somewhere, the SkyCamel had docked. A'Alhakoth didn't think SeekerStar was close enough for that short of a flight, so the aliens must have hauled their victims to their own ship, as a prelude to whatever it was they had planned.

Hopefully, she could find a beam weapon in here, somehow stashed by Erin or one of the others against just such an emergency. A knife wasn't going to do the trick, if she was surrounded by a mob of aliens that had the power to contain Daniel.

Again the complete silence was unnerving, even though she had heard Erin's voice talking to someone briefly. Both rear hatches beeped themselves open, so something was presumably happening.

A'Alhakoth counted to one hundred slowly. Twice.

She took a deep breath and tried to roll face down without moving the lid. That way, she could get her feet under her to stand, maybe to maneuver if she needed to.

If that would do her any good.

The lid was hinged. She pressed up slowly, stopping when

she had a crack of vision at the top.

Nothing. Several jumpseats had been left down, so somebody was going to catch hell for not following the Commander's rules, but it would be a minor infraction in the scheme of piracy and mental assault.

A'Alhakoth opened the lid the rest of the way and stood, stretching after the ride in a too-small box.

The SkyCamel was empty. She crept forward and confirmed that the front was as well, before peeking out the front portal.

Wait a minute. This is WinterStar's flight deck. What are we doing here?

She saw several figures moving away, towards the lift that carried people to the central core. Not all of them were human. Several looked like enormous, pink snakes.

What in the many hells had Daniel found?

Or who had found him?

She was at a crossroads. She could pursue them to the ship's core, or try to find if anything was left in the armory. Would they blow the ship up or steal it? Those were really the only two options, if you were going to ride the lifts into the zero-grav core of the vessel.

She seemed to remember that the skyvox didn't have that great of a range, considering where SeekerStar was floating, so calling Kathra was probably doomed to failure. That left her.

Without a weapon, there was little A'Ahlakoth could do, if those snakes had powers sufficient to overwhelm Daniel, so she set out looking for something. Anything. Even a handful of plumbing fixtures she could throw and a length of pipe would do.

A'Alhakoth checked her memory and headed right around the rim of the ship.

She didn't have much time.

FORTY-TWO

"Damn it," Kathra snarled as *WinterStar* blinked out of existence. "Do you have a track?"

"I do," Obioma replied.

Obioma was the actual pilot, while Ife handled all communications and sensors, and acted as the Commander for the regular crew when Kathra wasn't around.

"Where?" Kathra demanded.

Obioma turned and stared at her for a moment, with a look like she had bitten something sour.

"The Turtle," she finally admitted.

"Damn it," Kathra repeated. "Is Isaev clear?"

"Affirmative, Kathra," Ife spoke up now. "His shuttle has departed, headed to his factory, well out of our path."

"And Erin's SkyCamel docked with *WinterStar*?" she asked, mostly just to confirm.

"She did," Ife nodded "There were no further communications from that point."

"Jump as soon as the drives are charged," she ordered.

It was obvious. Daniel had met his match.

And fallen to them. Erin and the others had probably been little more than innocent bystanders at that point.

Now she would need to chase them, whoever it was, and stop them from…what?

SeekerStar lacked the weaponry necessary to destroy the Turtle. Even a Septagon had only pounded fruitlessly on that massive, green hull with its Ram Cannons. *WinterStar* wasn't even as heavily armed, with only two slightly-illegal Ram Cannon turrets, twinned at either end of the long axis, with lesser turrets around the larger rim.

What could someone who could fit into a SkyCamel do against that?

Besides stealing it.

Erin had warned her that someone would eventually find a way to overpower Daniel, but Kathra had not believed that was possible.

She had apparently been wrong.

"Contact A'Alhakoth and let her know she's on her own for now, and that we'll be back for her," Kathra ordered.

"I have been trying already, Kathra," Ife replied. "But I cannot find her signal on the station, or anywhere else."

"Was she with them?" Kathra asked, but that was a rhetorical question.

A'Alhakoth and Erin had worked out a plan of secrecy, so perhaps the young woman had found a way to sneak over to *WinterStar* with them. That, or she had also been captured.

Kathra ground her teeth and considered her options. One more Spectre wouldn't be all that useful on the other side, so she would command from here. And do whatever she needed to do.

Find whoever she needed to kill.

"Ready to jump," Obioma called out. "Initiating now."

SeekerStar leapt into the darkness.

FORTY-THREE

TRY AS HE MIGHT, Daniel could not break through the ice again. He was trapped, deep in his own mind, pushing and snapping at the bars the ishtan had erected, but nothing was working.

Time had passed. He wasn't sure how much, but enough. The *salauds* had taken him and the others to the core and then the bridge. There, they finally ran into someone. Daniel didn't know her by more than face and dietary preferences, but she turned into a glass-eyed zombie half a second after she turned her head towards them when the main hatch opened.

She had immediately programmed a jump, going to the place where Daniel had already shown them the Turtle was quietly waiting in space.

They had, as near as he could tell, arrived. It wasn't a long flight from here, but an hour had passed while he was contained in some fugue.

Deep in his soul, where he was hiding, Daniel had the faintest hope that the ishtan would take him over there and leave Erin and the others behind. Without him, there was nothing they could do that was a significant threat to the aliens.

Perhaps they would just kill him, steal the Turtle, and return whence they came? Could it be that easy?

But he found himself in the middle of a convoy, surrounded by the four women and then six pink snakes. Out into the corridor to the elevator ring. The chambers were large enough for such a group, except that Daniel had pink fur pressed against his back and legs as they rode down into gravity slowly.

He wished he could say or do anything about it, but he felt more like a disembodied ghost than anything. Presumably, a priest would come along soon and banish him back to whichever of the hells welcomed chefs masquerading as mad gods. Or vice versa.

They landed on the outer ring and circled to the flight deck in near silence. *WinterStar* had never been a particularly crowded vessel. Kathra kept the crew down to only those people who had proven themselves, rather than putting amateurs on this deck and hoping.

Still, completely empty was strange. He was used to seeing a few people headed off on some errand.

Empty as a graveyard.

Daniel wished he could take his mental images somewhere else, but his impending death just kept reaching up a cold hand and poking him in the kidneys.

The ishtan had chased Urid-Varg for however many thousand years, waiting until they could achieve their vengeance. Daniel had just killed the man first, and taken his place, as far as the snakes were concerned.

His evil would not stand.

He didn't have a really good argument against that. Most of what he did qualified as evil on some level. Upgrading the Mbaysey to a new ship had been a good deed, and even then he had tweaked and smothered overreactions from the Trade Factor during the negotiations.

Nothing bad, but keeping a lid on the usual explosions of personality. Drawing out contentment that this was a good enough deal and set him up for even greater things later when Kathra returned with other things to sell.

Things completely unique.

Daniel didn't understand how the valence drives worked, other than you opened a hole in reality and flew through to someplace that would take light-decades to cover.

At least two of the ships on the Turtle used something else. Not counting the turtle itself, which wasn't a machine so much as a sea creatures flying in the depths of space instead.

Onto the SkyCamel again. Everyone buckled in as Erin cleared the locks and backed them into the darkness.

Because it was automatic, Daniel had ended up in front, next to the tall cyborg as she flew. He would have liked to turn his head to study her profile. The barcode tattoo. The mohawk needing to be trimmed a little. Even the mechanical leg that said more about how tough and amazing she was as a pilot, that she could do all this with just one leg.

But he could not move. Not even his eyes more than enough to focus on things as they entered his field of vision.

The Star Turtle.

Bigger than a Septagon in length, but made of elegant, smooth lines, rather than the geometrically square edges of the great ships. He did not have the space for seventy decks, plus all the command towers, so he could never fit that many people inside, but he had forests and orchards. Alien bees like the masons he had enjoyed watching as a child in the garden, working their slow and careful way around the flowers as they filled up at the buffet.

Everyone thought mason bees were useless, since they didn't make enough excess honey to harvest, but Daniel understood the importance of working hard to help everyone, and that was what mason bees did. Pollinate. Provide beauty and food to the world.

How did he get there?

Ishtan. They had stirred up his memories in seeking his secrets. Old things were no longer buried under newer piles. He imagined that his nightmares would have been exquisite, to have so much new material to incorporate, but Daniel had no doubts that they would kill him when he was no longer useful.

Open the vessel, a voice from the heavens commanded him.

Daniel ignored it as just another nightmare made dayflesh.

Open the vessel, it repeated.

Daniel understood that the longest of the ishtan was addressing him. Commanding him.

Could they not command the Turtle? What an interesting concept.

He would not put it past that *salaud,* Urid-Varg, to have linked the command of the ship to something.

The gem, of course.

Only the bearer of the gem could issue orders. Urid-Varg never knew what his new horse would look like, so that was not enough. But imprinting the essence of the gem on the creature was, because that would always be how Urid-Varg was identified.

Even after Daniel had killed the son of a diseased camel.

He resisted. Tried to.

Mental tentacles grabbed hold of his mind and squeezed. Pain centers lit with hideous fire.

Daniel would have screamed, if it had been allowed.

Open the vessel.

He surrendered. Time had passed as he fought, but they

had spent hundreds of lifetimes patiently hunting their prey. They would outlast even an opinionated chef.

He reached out with his mind and told the nearest fin to admit them. Five other minds sat atop his as he did so, as he had once carried Kathra and the others when she executed Ugonna for that woman's treachery. These were poised to stop him from doing anything else, such as telling the Turtle to annihilate the SkyCamel in a blast of whatever those eyes generated.

Not that he hadn't considered it. Erin and the others didn't deserve such a death, but ending the ishtan would be doing the galaxy a favor, as near as he could tell. Especially if they decided to turn themselves into lesser versions of Urid-Varg.

Such evil will never be tolerated! that voice boomed painfully in his mind. *Never accepted.*

Daniel understood that he had no inner voice now. That someone was always in the room with him listening. Probably measuring out his burial shroud.

Hopefully they were serious about their definition of evil, although he had no idea where they might go, if their home and species were both destroyed.

Nobody offered an opinion, so presumably a worm like him didn't merit such.

In the distance, the fin of the Turtle split open like an oyster shell and lights came on.

FORTY-FOUR

Damn it. A'Alhakoth wanted to snarl the word at the top of her lungs, but it wouldn't do any good.

She'd been so busy paying attention to her search for anything she could use as a weapon that she'd lost track of Erin and the others.

At some point, they had emerged from the core and returned to the flight deck, while she'd been fixing herself a club.

The feel of a SkyCamel launching was specific. The whole hull rang as the hatches cycled. The Spectres were all much quieter, but only because you climbed down a ladder and sealed yourself up before simply detaching and letting the bigger ship throw you across space.

A'Alhakoth floated in the central core where the lifts all came together and cursed some more. All that, and she had failed. All the stalking slowly to get to the armory, only to discover it empty and stripped. Then to the machine shop, likewise empty, but she'd managed to detach a water pipe from a sink, so at least she had a club now.

Not much time had passed while she was working, but it had been too much.

They had done whatever it was they came to *WinterStar* for and then left.

Hopefully, they hadn't wired a bomb to blow the ship up in a few minutes. That might be a useful solution to her as a failure, but it wouldn't do anything to help Erin.

A'Alhakoth gripped a side bar and got her feet under her. If *under* had any meaning in zero gravity. She launched herself forward toward the navigating bridge.

A booby trap in engineering would be invisible to her, as she'd never been in the engine room of a major vessel before. But they had flown here, and she didn't think the pink aliens had been able to do that themselves, since they had needed Erin to fly the SkyCamel.

The command deck on *WinterStar* was arranged by someone used to thinking in gravity, even though this vessel didn't generate any. The deck was flat and square, when it could have just as easily been arranged all the way around the inner ring of the tube.

A'Alhakoth supposed that whoever had built it normally designed things for bigger ships, or maybe large chunks of *WinterStar* had been salvaged from a vessel with grav field inducers.

Five stations, all on a level plain as she entered almost sideways from her own relative down, like an aquatic mammal entering its dam. One woman sat perfectly still at the piloting station.

She found it spooky that the pilot didn't react at all to the sound of A'Alhakoth entering. Just sat there, staring ahead.

A'Alhakoth caught a stanchion with her free hand and shifted slowly to her left, keeping the club in her hand ready if she needed it.

Kamsichor Obiajunwa. That was the woman's name.

Older, as humans measured such things. Never a member of the comitatus, but good enough to sit watches on the bridge when Ife or Obioma weren't around. She had geometric designs cut into the short buzz of her hair.

She never moved.

A'Alhakoth had wondered if there was another snake still on *WinterStar*, controlling whichever women were here, but they should have found her. Heard her moving around and done something about it, so she presumed that they had all left on the SkyCamel with Erin and Daniel.

A'Alhakoth powered up one of the other stations, keeping an eye on Kamsichor, but the woman was oblivious to everything. The SkyCamel was making its way to the so-called Turtle.

Kanus didn't have such a creature in its biosphere, so she just had to guess what turtles apparently looked like, based on the monstrous thing floating off *WinterStar*'s bow. It certainly had the smooth streamlining of an aquatic creature. She presumed that the things sticking out at the corners and middle must be swimming limbs, with a head at the front and a tail at the rear.

The size boggled her mind. She had heard stories of the Sept Empire's enormous flagships, but Kanus barely built ships larger than *WinterStar*. And those used a grav field inducers similar to the human one, so a lot of the volume was power systems and equipment, with crew crammed in an uncomfortably tiny volume.

Until she had met the Commander, A'Alhakoth had never imagined just living in space and letting spin generate the equivalent of gravity for you.

She didn't dare scan anything, lest she warn the aliens that they had missed someone and they decide to come back for her. And the Commander wasn't here, so A'Alhakoth didn't know if her best course of action to take would involve opening fire on the SkyCamel right now and killing her comrades, as the best chance to eliminate the pink aliens.

Comitatus meant offering your life for Kathra Omezi and the others. Daniel seemed to be part of that group as well, as did the small woman Ndidi Zikora.

Small. Compared to the rest, perhaps. Daniel's height, so only half a head taller than A'Alhakoth, compared to the several heads taller of the Commander.

There were no good choices. A'Alhakoth made a list of bad ones and cursed herself for failing Erin and the others. Perhaps, she should have just stayed on the SkyCamel, and planned to jump out and attack someone in flight. Or followed them to the bridge unarmed and tried to do something.

Hadn't Daniel used a fire suppressor to kill a god?

She concentrated on breathing and studying the screen.

The SkyCamel approached the Star Turtle and one of the swimming limbs split along the horizontal axis, revealing a sort of flight deck, unto which they landed, with the thing closing up again like a mouth.

She decided to risk action at this point, hoping that whatever the aliens were doing over there would keep them too busy to watch *WinterStar*. She moved from her seat to hang in front of Kamsichor, more or less on her vertical.

A'Alhakoth reached out a hand and poked the woman in the shoulder with the hand not ready to swing her pipe. Her feet kept her from bouncing backwards as she gripped the hanging bar.

Kamsichor woke up. That was the only way A'Alhakoth could think of to describe the change in the woman's eyes. The pilot blinked several times and her eyes suddenly focused.

"What?" she said, but A'Alhakoth gestured her to silence.

She didn't think the pink snakes could hear, but feared

that any emotional spike in the aether might turn eyes this way.

"Aliens with powers like Daniel Lémieux's took over your mind, back in Tavle Jocia ," A'Alhakoth explained.

"Where are we then?" Kamsichor blinked too rapidly.

"Wherever it was you parked the Star Turtle," A'Alhakoth said. "We've come through jump and are sitting close by. All of the aliens, too. Erin, Daniel, Iruoma, Kam, and Nkechi over on the same SkyCamel that I stowed away on earlier."

"What are your orders?" Kamsichor perked up and studied her now.

Orders? I'm half your age, and a complete newcomer to the squadron who has only been here for six weeks!

But she was also comitatus. The Commander had tried to explain to a naïve A'Alhakoth what that really meant, but it hadn't hit home until now. If Kathra Omezi wasn't here, then Spectre Twenty-Three was in charge.

Frantically, she thought through everything Erin or one of the others had taught her about the Mbaysey and *WinterStar*.

And what Father had taught her about hunting. She needed to be a predator now, just as Erin and Daniel had become her prey.

"Passive scans only," A'Alhakoth ordered this older veteran in as firm a voice as a youngster like her could. "Confirm where we are, what status the ship is in, and prepare for a jump away if we need to chase the Turtle down."

Kamsichor nodded and began pressing buttons and typing commands.

Just like that.

That was what comitatus meant.

"One other thought," A'Alhakoth said. "Unlock the guns, in case we need to destroy the SkyCamel when it returns."

FORTY-FIVE

When she got loose from this, Erin was going to kill every one of those snakes. Skin the corpses and eat them, intelligent or otherwise. She would wear their fur as a jacket and make a career of hunting down any species that looked remotely like them and wiping it out as well, just in case.

Maybe she would ask Daniel for the coordinates to their planet of origin, and she'd try to convince Kathra to let her bomb it into a radioactive wasteland. Kathra probably wouldn't put up too much of a fuss after she heard the whole story.

They had worried about what Daniel might do. They should have known better. She'd been inside the chef's mind enough to understand.

These fuckers were going to be chicken fingers when she was done with them. The comitatus would feast on their flesh and then their souls, because if Erin understood the memories that had flown back and forth like water around her, the gem Daniel wore came from the oldest grandpapa snake ever, and all the rest of these pikers together barely had enough power combined to hold her, the women, and Daniel.

What could she and Kathra do, if they had access to such gems as she was happy to cut out of corpses?

Erin was going to kill all of them and then find out.

The *salaud* in her mind had made her fly over to the Turtle. After a messy battle with Daniel, he had opened the landing fin and she had put the ship down as close to the inner hatch as she could without getting fancy.

Everything was closed up now and the SkyCamel shut down. One by one, the snakes forced them out onto the deck, and five of them slithered along in a circle around Daniel, with the last one working overtime to keep the four of them in line.

Quiet didn't mean quiescent, you son of a bitch.

They approached the airlock and entered the vast space Daniel liked to joke about holding musical concerts in, one of these days. Then into the hangar where Urid-Varg had kept all the old shuttles and ships he had stolen, minus the four that Kathra had sold to that *Anglo* at Tavle Jocia.

The Star Turtle was a huge beast of a ship, in three major decks that all had vaulted ceilings. The conqueror himself had tucked personal quarters forward near the head, in a section of the neck where it all pinched down and he lived like a damned mendicant monk, raw stone walls, thin sleeping pad, and not much more.

To get there, everybody had to traverse a couple of brag halls filled with trophies, and not just the shuttles inside the bay, but that stupid hall of skulls where previous victims had been stored, stripped of all flesh and preserved.

Talk about sick and morbid. It wasn't even like the *salaud* ever had company to be impressed by such things. No, this was just a male and his typical dick-measuring competitions with everyone else. As if a dick was the measure of a male.

It was, however, a pretty good reason so few of them were kept around. After all, Kathra and the tribe only needed the product of the balls, and not the delivery mechanism.

Erin tried to pay attention to the skulls as they walked through the place, but didn't remember anything like a giant snake. Only skulls that were close enough to human in shape and sensory apparatus, horns or not. Maybe he had never ridden the snakes, and only kept the people who had the privilege of wearing that ugly lime suit.

Let me roll my eyes at your stupid ghost, Urid-Varg.

None of the snakes seemed all that interested in the skulls, except to buzz angrily around her head where she could taste the conversation, but not actually hear the words. Like maybe they didn't like that old shit any more than the rest of them did, but Erin had the feeling that they weren't content in knowing that the *salaud* was roasting in hell now.

Seemed from the flavor of things that Daniel was on the list to go with him. If that was the case, they probably should have killed him as soon as they hit the system, because eventually someone would get tired. Or stop paying close enough attention.

Something.

Erin couldn't do anything, but waited like a big, black cat, poised up in a tree as she listened to something coming down the trail.

There was going to be a pounce, just as soon as she was free.

FORTY-SIX

Daniel fought, but there was nothing he could do now to break through the ice to where the ishtan were protected from his rage. He had surprised them the once, but they understood how he had done it, perhaps, and could thwart him.

Step by step, they walked him to the bridge of the Star Turtle. He could taste the awe in their voices at the vessel that Urid-Varg had stolen somewhere. The ishtan had nothing at all like it, having been a largely planet-bound species, even at their height, unlike the humans who explored every which way given any chance.

But he was their enemy. And they were his now.

He could hear his impending doom, but they had to first account for the Turtle, and Daniel had not stolen the right memories from the creatures to understand how they planned to do that.

He could only walk.

The bridge was crowded when everyone arrived. He was so used to sitting alone up here, or perhaps one other person, if Kathra or Ndidi happened to join him for a flight. Now he had four human women, all bigger than him, and the six ishtan snakes, currently coiled and upright around him.

Open the window, the leader commanded.

Daniel did not resist greatly. This wasn't a battle worth fighting, as he sought to conserve his strength for some coming conflagration.

Around him, large sections of the head bridge turned transparent, showing the distant stars and the bulk of *WinterStar* parked close.

Daniel doubted that the miniscule crew could do anything, even if they weren't under ishtan control. Even Septagon Uwalu had only been able to punch him lightly with their Ram Cannons while he had avoided the monstrous beam that emerged from the bow.

Would the four women be allowed to return home, once Daniel was dead? Would the ishtan kill him and the Turtle, and turn pirate by keeping *WinterStar*?

They would be in for a monumental surprise if they did that, since most of its crew was gone, over on SeekerStar.

Would Kathra understand what had happened? And would she pursue them, or take the opportunity to be rid of Daniel's problems forever?

He doubted it, even if the four women were comitatus-sworn and expected to give up their lives for the Commander. Kathra would see someone stealing her old ship as an insult too great to accept, and SeekerStar had the firepower to defeat and destroy *WinterStar*, if it came to that.

A new flight vector appeared in Daniel's mind as someone forced him to sit on the cold, stone throne. Contact wasn't necessary, except as it helped him center his mind to go flying.

They were going to fly Daniel and his Star Turtle into the nearby star and use that to destroy both and end his evil. The thing didn't even have a name, as it was just a cool, orange dwarf without any planetary disk, so nothing that the Mbaysey or anyone else had ever been interested in exploiting.

Just a string of numbers and letters.

Fitting, perhaps, for a ghost like Urid-Varg and all his legacy to die.

Now you need to die, the snake snarled into his head.

Daniel decided he had had enough. They couldn't just reach in and take control of his mind and body, like he could do to others. It would be necessary to force him onto a path, diving the Turtle into a star already relatively nearby.

Would they force one of the women to shoot him while he fought the other ishtan off? That might explain why they had brought them here, while leaving the other crew on *WinterStar*, although that was just speculation.

Five minds landed on his back and tried to drive him under the water, to hold him there where he might drown. A tendril of thought escaped his control and touched the Turtle. Daniel felt the beast began to move under the guidance of mental hands no longer his.

His death would be here shortly. He didn't know if they intended to join him, but he was going down fighting.

FORTY-SEVEN

KATHRA HAD NOT LEFT the bridge of SeekerStar during the short flight, just as she was sure that all of her women were currently strapped into their Spectres and waiting for emergence on the far side, so they could blast into the darkness for whatever battle they might fight, against whoever had taken Erin and Daniel against their will.

"Counting down, Commander," Ife brought her attention to the big screen currently only showing the strange darkness between universes.

"All guns live," Kathra said. "All Spectres prepare for battle."

Acknowledgements flooded in. Kathra wasn't surprised, but this would be more than just chasing off some pirates, or giving the finger to a Sept Patrol as the squadron danced away into the darkness.

They would emerge on the far side of the Turtle, hoping to catch everyone off-guard by deliberately flying long. She had the Ram Cannons to destroy her old ship if she needed to.

Nothing could kill the Turtle, as far as Kathra knew, but if she couldn't claim *WinterStar*, nobody else would either.

The dropped into space from the jump and landed long and silent.

"Status?" Kathra turned her attention to Ife.

"The Turtle is still there," her bridge commander never looked up from her screens. "*WinterStar* as well. The turtle is starting to move, but the course makes no sense."

"Show me," Kathra ordered.

She considered the screen from over Ife's shoulder.

No, that made perfect sense, if you wanted to dive into the center of the star to destroy yourself.

"Message from *WinterStar*, Commander," Ife suddenly perked up. "Narrow-beam-laser. A'Alhakoth is on the bridge in command."

A'Alhakoth?

It didn't make any sense, but it at least gave her someone over there she could rely on. And a warrior. Not all of the bridge crews had that combativeness built in.

"Follow-up message," Ife continued. "Scout team captured by pink snake aliens. Erin, Daniel, and the other three took a SkyCamel onto the Turtle with the snakes without realizing A'Alhakoth was on the ship. She's been organizing and awaiting developments."

Yes, like what could a tiny ship like *WinterStar* do against a Star Turtle?

"Tell her good job and stand by," Kathra said. "Both ships to pace the Turtle, but remain behind it and away from the forward beams. Scan for any shuttles or other craft leaving one of the flight fins and lock weapons on it immediately, but not to fire until ordered."

Kathra watched the Turtle come smoothly about. She had no idea how resistant that hull was to heat, but

SeekerStar would only be able to pursue for a short period of time before needing to swing around, stop, and accelerate away.

Something would have to happen shortly.

She just wasn't sure what it would be.

FORTY-EIGHT

"Naupati, we'll be emerging in thirty seconds."

Pasdar nodded to himself and returned to his seat at the rear of the Great Causeway, planting himself next to Rostami, who maintained a serious mien, even with a hint of a smile in his eyes.

"All weapons charged and unlocked, Naupati," Rostami said just loud enough to be heard.

Pasdar nodded. It had come down to this.

And they would probably only get one chance.

"GunMaster, you are to take command and align Vorgash with the Turtle as soon as we emerge," Pasdar ordered, catching the flinch in the man's shoulders as the implications dawned on him. "You will fire the Axial Megacannon as soon as you have a confirmed firing solution."

Most men would flinch. The GunMaster would command the entirety of the Septagon for those seconds, bending all other men to his will so that he could unleash destruction on his own, rather than being ordered to by a naupati.

Any mistakes would probably end his career.

On any other Septagon, that is. Pasdar understood that the creature had evaded Uwalu while the chain of orders slowly worked their way down the staff before any fire.

That had been too long. Pasdar would rather an aggressive man take a poorer shot, as long as he hit, rather than waiting so long that the creature spun like a bird and departed laughing.

Or whatever it was that the thing had done to Uwalu. Even the scientists were still unsure.

If they could wound the creature, Pasdar was willing to lose all trace of the Mbaysey for now while he hunted the Turtle, visions of angry white whales dancing at the edge of his vision.

He would succeed.

Vorgash returned to the universe.

"Target identified," a voice called out over the eruption of noise and chaos that always accompanied emergence into battle.

"Hard about starboard," the GunMaster snarled. "Bow down and engines prepare for maximum thrust. All generators go to redline immediately and hold there until countermanded."

Pasdar nodded. He even let Rostami see his emotions. The GunMaster was taking a very aggressive approach, but that was always better than a timid one. Letting the man have the ultimate responsibility would probably prove to be a good choice. If not, Pasdar would determine his fate only after the battle had been fought.

Outside the forward portals, stars began to shift as the mighty Septagon pivoted slowly on ice and began to draw forward. So much mass did not accelerate quickly, but the Turtle was caught in the middle of a turn, and could not make a translight leap to escape, with its beak pointed directly at the nearby star.

Pasdar could not think of a more foolish maneuver the aspbad over there could have chosen, even without expecting an ambush.

"Fire now!" the GunMaster yelled.

The forward portals automatically dimmed and shadowed as the Axial Megacannon erupted, a coherent beam of lased energy forty meters across and carrying enough destructive energy to destroy cities at the bottom of an atmosphere if necessary.

Like a knight's lance, it leapt out, catching the Turtle in the hindquarters on the starboard side hard enough that Pasdar could see it stagger as the energy of the beam was liberated on that unscannable, green shell in a cloud of plasma generated by hull plates melting.

"Again," the GunMaster ordered. "Divert all energy to the Megacannon to recharge, including life support systems. We can survive a few minutes on still air."

Pasdar considered intervening, but the first shot had been true, a harpoon into the beast's flank. And if it shaved time off the thirty-five to forty seconds needed to recharge the weapon, that might be worth it for the second shot. He would step in at that point and bring order before the GunMaster did any permanent damage to the vessel.

"Command Node, we have identified two other vessels pursuing the target," someone called. "Confirm the Mbaysey vessel *WinterStar* and the second vessel we identified departing Tavle Jocia. Tentative transponder code SeekerStar."

In his excitement, Pasdar had forgotten that this was all part of a stern chase of Kathra Omezi as well. Capturing or killing her would be even better, but only a bonus after killing the Turtle.

"Any other vessels in scanner range?" Rostami asked in a loud voice.

Yes, what about the Mbaysey? Pasdar doubted that the squadron would be located here, since this system was known to be a solitary star floating alone in space, probably ejected from some binary or trinary system in the recent past.

"Negative, Commanders," came the reply. "Only three vessels in range."

"Open fire on *WinterStar* with secondary armaments," Rostami ordered after a moment to check.

He and Pasdar had an almost telepathic communication link, these days. They would ignore the other ship, at least until it made the mistake of fighting back.

"All Patrols attack the Turtle," Pasdar commanded. "Maximum effort."

Again, Kathra Omezi was nothing that the Sept could not annihilate. It was her alien allies that needed to be neutralized as quickly as possible.

Out of the darkness, vessels began to accelerate. Pasdar rose again and began to pace, letting his view from the front of the Great Causeway give him the show of the smaller vessels racing ahead from all around Vorgash. They lacked even Ram Cannons, but could pound any small vessel to scrap quickly. Here, they would just pour fire into the already-wounded hull of the Turtle and do internal damage until the thing surrendered.

Or died.

FORTY-NINE

Daniel screamed in agony. Someone had just stabbed him in the kidneys with a powered knife and was trying to remove his spleen with it.

Except he was still seated atop Urid-Varg's command throne, resting his shoulder blades against the green stone.

For the briefest moment, the ishtan lost control of his mind, and Daniel was able to expand his senses outward.

The Turtle was on a path that would slam it into the atmosphere of a star hot enough to kill even something this tough, but he had time to turn away yet.

Behind him, *WinterStar* trailed in his wake, with a welcome SeekerStar behind that, surrounded by a swarm of Spectres, all still keeping their distance, as the star was a large blot in the skies ahead of them.

But another problem emerged.

Septagon Vorgash, the first of its type he had ever encountered, had arrived. Was here. Now.

Daniel had no idea how they had found him, or even what they were doing so deep into Free Worlds space, but the ship practically yelled its name on the psychic bands he could hear.

The pain in his back was from the Turtle. Vorgash had struck with the Axial Megacannon. He had been right to fear such a weapon at Azgon, when Uwalu had thought to do the same.

The blow was not mortal, but the Turtle might require decades to scar over the gash in the carapace that the weapon had inflicted.

Daniel could hear the crew of Vorgash celebrating, and preparing another shot. If the second struck in the same place as the first, it might gut the Turtle like a boning knife.

He tried to roll, and the ishtan stopped him. Six minds piled onto his, holding his mental hands short of the word that would bring the next shot onto unscarred hull.

Daniel screamed with the pain of the knife in his back and the rage of the creatures threatening his mind and his soul.

It took six of them to hold him. Contain him. Stop him.

That was their mistake.

Another scream of rage erupted, but this one was physical, rather than mental.

Surprise followed in its wake.

Daniel's eyes happened to be facing the correct direction to follow the action. Everything moved suddenly in slow motion.

Around him, six ishtan had taken up stations, four in the corners and two on the sides of the throne.

Four comitatus warriors had been largely moved into a corner and ignored, their captors content that the women were no longer a threat.

That was only a valid assumption when it only took five snakes to hold an angry chef. The sixth had turned and added his weight, in that moment when Daniel might have broken from their control again. They had held him.

Iruoma's scowl was a thing of serene beauty in Daniel's mind. Her rage was as great as his, at least.

She broke *free*.

The others were still bound, mentally trapped, just as Iruoma had been. Their anger was a background scent coming in from the window. Iruoma's rage was a grease fire erupting in the middle of the stove right in front of you. It would not be contained.

They turned to capture her again, but Daniel grabbed them in turn. He couldn't hold them long.

He didn't have to.

Iruoma erupted.

A hand flashed to a pistol, drew, fired. It was over so quickly that Daniel nearly missed it, even looking right at the goddess of destruction herself.

But suddenly only five minds held him.

He snarled and wrapped mental arms around the five. He didn't have to hold them long. Just hold them.

Iruoma slew a second ishtan with her beam.

Four.

You can't stop me now.

He reached out to crush the four remaining when his mind exploded.

FIFTY

"WHAT IN THE hells of Grish is that thing?" A'Alhakoth yelled at Kamsichor as the side of the Turtle erupted in a massive fireball.

Around her, the hull of *WinterStar* began to rock and thump with energy. She had never been in a space battle before, but A'Alhakoth's teen daydreams recognized the setting she had blundered into.

"The Septagon is firing on us," Kamsichor called back, frantically pushing buttons. "Several Patrols are in flight, but currently aiming themselves at the Turtle."

A'Alhakoth had the impression that this should be a job for half a dozen women, but there was nothing she could do to help right now.

Except give orders. Kamsichor Obiajunwa had a frantic look in her eyes when she glanced up.

"Open fire on the Septagon," she said with a quick gulp. "Who else is aboard?"

"Adanne is aft in engineering," Kamsichor barked back as her hands started to fly across various controls. "We can't stand against a Septagon. We're not powerful enough, even if we weren't short-handed."

"No, but we can distract it from attacking the Turtle or SeekerStar," A'Alhakoth said simply. "Is there anything aboard that needs to be removed before we end up being destroyed in battle?"

"Our lives," the woman said.

"Maybe," A'Alhakoth countered with a snarl. "*Comitatus.* If we have to die, then we make sure we charge them a damned high price."

The older woman laughed, and suddenly the hull of the Septagon glowed as one of the turrets scored a hit. A'Alhakoth had no idea what they might do against a small city in space, but she had taken an oath.

"Message from Kathra," Kamsichor said.

"*WinterStar*, what are you doing?" the Commander asked in a sharp tone.

"Fighting," A'Alhakoth said. "You should withdraw while you can."

Around her, the hull thumped again and again as the big ship found the range. How much damage the ship could take, she had no idea. Kamsichor was probably just as much at sea.

Nothing in A'Alhakoth's studies had suggested that the Mbaysey had ever fought a pitched battle against any force capable of standing. Just pirates they chased off, or Patrols they fled from.

Today would be different.

The hull rang.

"*WinterStar*, you have command of rescue operations," Kathra suddenly said.

It took A'Alhakoth a moment to understand what the Commander was saying. SeekerStar and the Spectres couldn't do anything against a force like this.

Except die.

Kathra Omezi had survived as long as she had by understanding when to run away. The Mbaysey as a tribe was more important than its members. Either here or those over on the Star Turtle. The Star Tribe needed to survive.

More bangs. Lights sputtered and recovered a moment later.

"What's the Septagon doing?" A'Alhakoth asked.

"Firing on us," Kamsichor said. "All the Patrols are firing into the Turtle. The Axial Megacannon has fired twice and hit both times. Recharging now."

"Can you reach anyone on the Turtle?" A'Alhakoth asked.

She knew she risked overloading Kamsichor, but she didn't know how to do it herself.

If she lived through this, the first thing she was doing was qualifying to sit on the bridge and fly and fight SeekerStar.

If she lived through this.

"Negative," Kamsichor said. Her voice got a melodic lilt when she was stressed.

"How are we doing?" she asked.

"The Ram Cannons have not lined us up yet," Kamsichor turned a dread smile over her shoulder at her. "We won't survive long when they do."

"Die well, *WinterStar*," Commander Omezi's voice came over the line.

"SeekerStar is away," Kamsichor said.

Something in one of the other consoles shorted, throwing sparks and smoke into the air. A'Alhakoth grabbed a fire suppressor immediately at hand and shot across the space, even as the hull rocked from a mightier blow.

"Ram Cannons," Kamsichor said grimly.

A'Alhakoth understood now what she meant. Those would destroy the ship.

Comitatus.

She had taken an oath, and death was included in the possible outcomes, but no daughter of Kanus was a coward. Certainly not her.

"Change course to ram the Septagon," A'Alhakoth ordered the woman. "Maximum speed."

FIFTY-ONE

MUCH AS SHE WANTED TO, Erin couldn't kill those stupid snakes. The rage and pain Daniel was broadcasting was almost enough to overwhelm her. The snakes were screaming in an entirely different manner. Loss and retribution, but they had also taken advantage of the chaos to flee.

None of the hatchways had been closed, looking at the hallway where the snakes had fled.

Most of the snakes. Two of them were charred hunks of carcass.

Daniel collapsed finally, his throat screamed dry and maybe bloody from the sounds that had come out of it.

Nothing Erin had ever heard in her life had prepared her for his shrieks. It was worse when they were inside her head, and she couldn't do anything to block her ears.

Kam was flat on her face. Nkechi was down to one knee like Erin. Only Iruoma was still standing, however wobbly that woman was.

"Daniel," Erin stagger-crawled to where he was laying.

She rolled him onto his side, just to confirm that the chef

was still alive after all that. Breath rattled around his chest, and his pupils reacted when she peeled open an eye.

The screaming was most gone, but around her, the hull of the Star Turtle boomed like a thousand drummers bashing away with mallets.

Iruoma moved to the door.

"No farther," Erin managed to gasp at the woman.

Iruoma scowled at her, but held her peace, that deadly pistol aimed outwards like a hunting dog sniffing for a trace.

Erin pinched Daniel's ear. Nothing. She slapped at his face a couple of times, more love-taps than anything. He stirred enough to open unfocusing eyes in her direction.

"What's happening?" she found herself yelling, as if he had gone deaf.

Or she had.

He mumbled something, so she put her ear next to his mouth.

"Septagon," he repeated in a breathy whisper.

Ah. That was the genesis of all this. Must have shot the Star Turtle with their city-killing cannon. Twice. And they had all survived.

She wasn't sure how much longer, though. Or how they would escape.

Could those snakes open the fin and escape in her SkyCamel? She was already set to kill them all. Piracy would just make it legal in any court with jurisdiction.

"Escape," Daniel said.

She wasn't sure if he was asking or ordering. Didn't have time to ask either, as he screamed for a third time and passed out.

Around her, the lights dimmed, like the ship had suffered a power failure.

They had to leave right now, if they were going to. Even a Star Turtle could apparently be killed by the Sept.

She was just sad that she didn't have time to cut apart one or the other of the corpses and bring that stupid gem along. But it would take more time than they had.

This was going to hurt. She rose and pulled Daniel more or less upright.

"Here," Iruoma stepped in and lifted the small male warrior over her shoulder.

Nkechi had Kam more or less awake and upright. About as good as the worst pub crawl they had ever managed, and maybe a little more past that.

They made it as far as the hatch. Iruoma had Daniel's weight, and still drew her pistol, intend on leading. Erin staggered in her wake, making sure that the other two didn't fall behind, no matter how many walls the three of them had to bounce off of.

The thunder outside had turn to hail, except they weren't on the surface of a planet where ice could fall on you. In space, such things were fragile puffs of solar wind and dreams, rather than punishing things.

More lights went out, but there were enough to navigate. They got back down the gullet of the beast and to the point where they would turn left and cross through the forests and the skull trophies, but Daniel roused himself and thumped Iruoma on the bottom enough to get her attention.

He turned them to the right instead, towards the older section of the Turtle, where some of the most bizarre designs had been stored. The oldest ones, too.

Things flown by creatures only vaguely human in size and shape.

A massive thump and all the lights failed. Gravity did, too.

Erin wondered if the Turtle itself had just died, or been knocked out.

It did make it easier to carry Daniel and the others along, when they could push him and pull the others.

He remained in a state somewhere just above dreaming. Lucid hallucinations that he shared with them, the kind that mostly aligned with the reality of the hallways around them, as he kept directing them out and down. This side was nearly a perfect copy of the other, but showed halls where a crew might have lived, had Urid-Varg ever desired one, or Kathra Omezi allowed it.

They got to the door of the number three flight bay. Iruoma managed to bring Daniel around enough that he could open the door and they entered into the most bizarre fairy wonderland ever. Most of these ships weren't steel and electronics. A few might have been organic. One of them reminded Erin of ice carved from the face of a glacier.

"Which one?" Iruoma asked Daniel, apparently understanding that he had brought them here on purpose.

The ships were locked to the deck, so they hadn't floated when the Turtle lost gravity. That was the only thing that would save them now, assuming he could open the fin and those Sept *salauds* either missed it, or tried to capture them.

Erin wasn't going to be taken alive. Not by them.

Daniel brought his mind back into the present from whatever nightmare he had been trapped in. Erin watched the pain of a human being dismembered alive recede from his eyes just long enough for him to point.

In the distance, one of the ships lit up. Erin had always wondered if that one was made of glass. It had that look, and the skin had the texture, but it wasn't transparent, and it apparently flew in space. She imagined a bunch of hexagonal rods stacked on top of each other, like an even larger hexagon band held them in place. Each of the rods was about a meter and a half, and the ship was nearly sixty long, but didn't have any sort of thruster nozzles or anything that marked even one end from the other.

Still, it seemed to be what Daniel needed. They moved.

He had stopped screaming. The noise of the hail blasting the hull had fallen almost to nothing as well.

Erin assumed that a Septagon was about to pounce on them, and they had minutes before the end.

Hopefully, this huge hunk of glass sculpture had a gun on it.

FIFTY-TWO

"SHEER OFF!" Pasdar ordered at the top of his lungs, uncaring who executed the order, as long as someone did. "All weapons concentrate on *WinterStar* and destroy it before it destroys us."

Never in his career had someone decided to actually ram a Septagon. But these rats had been backed into a corner, and he understood that sometimes, that was the risk.

Vorgash had pounded the vessel mercilessly with the Ram Cannons. The outer ring had stopped spinning, and in a few places large chunks had been blown off of it. But the ship had been set on a course while it had power, and a Septagon was a huge beast to turn, even at the best of times.

This was not the best of times.

In less than four minutes, the sparking, semi-destroyed remains of Kathra Omezi's flagship would slam into the side of Vorgash like a knife entering his kidneys. Just as he had done to the Star Turtle earlier.

"Is there any way to avoid it?" Rostami called to the twenty men frantically trying to prevent catastrophe.

One head turned and Pasdar watched a man's lips purse,

as though he was about to turn his own wife in for treason. Surely, it couldn't be that bad, could it?

"Speak," Pasdar ordered the man, walking closer.

"We could jump, Naupati," the officer said grimly. "The drives are charged and we could zero a safe enough course to move several light-years away. Our prey might escape by the time we could calculate a return, but we avoid a collision now."

He hung his head, as though he expected to have it struck from his shoulders for such a cowardly suggestion. Pasdar made a note to have a long conversation with Rostami and his top forty or so aides about speaking and thinking more flexibly, at least while he was in command of this ship.

Another naupati might have the man killed in the most painful method anyone could devise. But the officer was also about to save all of their lives.

"Calculate a blind jump and execute it!" Pasdar yelled, confused at this moment as to which men he should even be looking at. "Better to survive to fight again than die stupidly. Do it."

The day had already turned far and away from anything his entire career had prepared him for. The Turtle might be dead now. Certainly, it had ceased broadcasting any detectable signals after the third shot from the Axial Megacannon had slammed into it. It was slowly tumbling as well.

And the fools had been caught in a turn. The star itself would capture the vessel in another twelve hours at the most, melting it and destroying whatever alien allies Omezi had found.

He would defeat her yet. Perhaps the day after tomorrow, instead of today, but Vorgash had to survive intact, in order to bring Sept law to the uncivilized parts of the galaxy.

Off his bow, *WinterStar* charged like a blind buck, intent

on goring her pursuer one last time before dying. His guns had fallen silent as the range got too close. Pasdar presumed her guns had died when generators or engines had cut out.

The wreckage or the pieces would still enter Vorgash like a knife.

Except the Septagon leapt suddenly into the darkness.

Naupati Amirin Pasdar let go a breath he had been unaware he had been holding.

Even a short jump would take time to overcome. The Septagon had inertia that needed to be killed. The ship had to come about and recalculate a safe distance to arrive from the hopeful corpse of the Star Turtle.

An hour would pass, but SeekerStar had previously leapt away with no indication that it was returning, just as his gunners had come to realize that Omezi was on the other ship and before they could adjust their aim at the newcomer.

Run. I will yet catch you.

"Well done," Pasdar called loud enough to overcome the buzzing of the men in his Command Node. "You have killed our target and saved the Septagon from serious damage. Let no man cast aspersions on your honor or your courage, gentlemen. Now, the next challenge awaits, as we must return before they can all escape us."

He sat and let the adrenaline burn itself out as below him his men went to work.

FIFTY-THREE

"Enough," A'Alhakoth ordered Kamsichor. "Call Adanne and tell her to meet us on the cargo deck. We must abandon ship now."

Kamsichor looked like she had aged a decade in the last fifteen minutes, but the woman had shown as much bravery as any person A'Alhakoth had ever met.

They abandoned the bridge together and thrust their flight down the long axis of the ship like fish swimming upstream. The outer ring of *WinterStar* had stopped spinning at some point. A'Alhakoth wasn't even sure how much of it had been blasted clear by the Septagon's guns. Certainly, most of the women out there would have been killed had there been any.

But she and the other two women had done their duty. Now, to see if they could survive it.

Firing had ceased. The hull still popped and rang, but those were fires and explosions rattling the ship itself as systems failed. Very little of the damage was on the central hull, other than the front sections that had been shattered by fire. The forward turret was a crater, as well as the generators servicing it and most of the forward crew quarters, but those were all as thankfully empty as the outer ring had been.

Down the central shaft they shot. A'Alhakoth caught sight of Adanne coming forward from where she had been shepherding her engines.

Thank the very gods that the Patrol craft had all been chasing after the Turtle. By the time anyone realized that *WinterStar* was a threat, they had all flown past at such a speed that they would be too late to turn around and kill their own mad speed, to say nothing of returning to shoot this ship from the rear.

A'Alhakoth went in first, diving into the one SkyCamel stored on the cargo deck, instead of along the outer ring, for those times you needed to move heavy cargo and didn't want to do it in gravity.

She had not yet qualified on the Spectres, but a SkyCamel was a much easier beast to fly.

"Strap yourselves in," she called as she powered systems up and skipped large chunks of the preflight checklist.

They needed to be gone as soon as they cleared the hull or they were dead. And needed to be clear as soon as she could bring things to readiness.

"Go!" Kamsichor yelled after a few seconds.

Rather than look, A'Alhakoth triggered the systems that would open the locks holding this SkyCamel in place.

Nothing happened.

Too much damage, perhaps? The systems should have been proof against a power failure, running on localized batteries as a redundancy, but they held her to the hull, where she was minutes from slamming into the giant warship and dying an explosive and messy death.

"What's wrong?" Adanne called.

"Locks won't release!" A'Alhakoth yelled back at her. "We're stuck. Suggestions?"

"Overload your engines," Adanne said in a clear and concise suggestion of utter insanity. "Use all your maneuvering thrusters as well."

"Why?" A'Alhakoth had to ask, completely lost now.

"The arms are not that strong, Spectre Twenty-Three," Adanne replied in a stern, commanding voice. "They are designed to capture and hold a SkyCamel floating nearby, not one resisting. Plus, Kathra will not dock your pay for breaking them off right now. At least not any worse than she will for killing her ship."

Chuckles all around. What was the worst the Commander could do, sentence her to death? If she didn't break clean shortly, Kathra Omezi would have to climb down into hell herself to handle the task.

A'Alhakoth double-checked her fuel feeds and temperatures, and then began to pour power into the systems. She had to keep everything balanced, so that she had some control if she did this, or she'd slam the SkyCamel into the side of the ship as she maneuvered. Or the Septagon.

Nothing.

More power.

She grabbed the flight yoke in a death grip and thumbed the engines wide open. The hull began to groan. Or maybe that was her nerves screaming at the stress.

Father had trained her to be as much a warrior as any of her brothers. Daniel and Erin had weighed her very soul and recommended her to the Commander.

Kathra Omezi had made her *comitatus*.

She would not fail.

Something broke aft.

It wasn't the bending of metal turning under torque. One of the arms failed and broke, maybe somewhere around the wrist.

The SkyCamel lurched and A'Alhakoth fought the

controls to keep her nose aligned with the blackness ahead, rather than swinging on a hinge and slamming into *WinterStar* with power.

A second docking arm began to bow under the pressure, like a leash extending as the SkyCamel tried to drag *WinterStar* itself over to an interesting bush to sniff.

A'Alhakoth took a breath and jerked the yoke hard right and then immediately left.

The SkyCamel jolted like a dog shaking off water and broke free.

Someone yelled. Howled with joy. Maybe all of them.

A'Alhakoth left the engines going full tilt, unknowing how big an explosion it would trigger when *WinterStar* hit the gigantic intruder and unwilling to be anywhere close when that happened.

She did turn on all the sensors this poor tub had, blind and feeble as they were. At least the collision alarms were good ones.

A'Alhakoth's mouth fell open as she looked at the screen.

The Septagon was gone. Vanished. *WinterStar* was flying into nothingness.

Well, not nothing, they were too close to the star, and on a slowly-intercepting vector. The gravity would pull the ship down into the stellar forge soon enough, unless someone brought a huge towtruck to this system to save it, and she couldn't envision anybody wanting to try that hard.

WinterStar was broken. Murdered, but she had died heroically, especially if the Septagon had fled rather than be rammed. All of the Patrol vessels had left as well.

The SkyCamel was alone, with *WinterStar* and Daniel's Star Turtle. A'Alhakoth checked the flight vectors and confirmed the second problem. The snakes had set it on a course directly into the face of the sun. It would splash in twelve or maybe eighteen hours at the longest, destroying the vessel presumably, and all the treasures that she had only heard about from Kam and Ndidi.

That ship might be older than written records on Kanus, and it would be gone. Already, the craft had a noticeable tumble, plus the three terrible wounds in the shell that had killed it.

A light appeared on the far edge of the ship. Detached itself and moved away. Not directly towards her SkyCamel, but closer.

"Kamsichor, I need you up here now!" A'Alhakoth yelled.

"What's happening?" the woman unbuckled herself and flowed forward to the co-pilot's seat.

"We're unarmed," A'Alhakoth said. She pointed at the screen and the image out the window. "And I don't care to know what that thing is. You need to plot us a course to the Concursion so we can get away."

"Kathra always required three lags in an approach," Kamsichor said as she powered her own systems live. "That way, she cannot be followed."

"Whatever you need to do," A'Alhakoth said. "Plot us an away and go."

"Understood."

Thank the gods that Kathra had refit several of her SkyCamels with petite valence drives while she was at Tavle Jocia. That would save their lives right now.

"SkyCamel Nine, what is your status?" a voice suddenly came over the radio.

Was that Erin?

"This is SkyCamel Nine," A'Alhakoth replied as Kamsichor's face lit up with excitement.

But the other woman didn't know about the mind-controlling snakes.

A'Alhakoth opened her engines a little and pushed the bow away from an intercept with that beacon of light moving through space. She had no idea what sort of range the pink snakes could mind-grab you, and didn't care to get any closer than she had to.

"A'Alhakoth, this is Erin, Iruoma, Kam, Nkechi, and Daniel," the voice continued. "Those *salauds* killed the Turtle and we're making our escape in one of Daniel's weirder shuttle craft."

"And your friends?" A'Alhakoth asked.

"Iruoma killed two of them in the fracas," Erin said. "The others tucked tail and fled. They might be still stuck on the Turtle, unless they can figure out how to open the flight deck. Where's our other friend?"

"I tried to fly *WinterStar* into the Septagon," A'Alhakoth laughed with an edge of hysteria. "Well, Kamsichor did. I think they jumped to light-speed to escape. All their hunting dogs apparently went with them, but I expect everyone to return once they can. Does your ship had valence drives?"

"According to Daniel, something close enough," Erin replied.

"We were about to plot a path to Concursion," A'Alhakoth said carefully.

Somewhere, the rest of the Mbaysey tribal squadron was waiting to meet them. A'Alhakoth had only heard stories about the ships. All the ClanStars. The two *WaterStars*. *IronStar*. *ForgeStar*.

Hopefully, the Commander would be waiting for them to arrive, and not too badly put out at what A'Alhakoth had chosen to do, when it came time for a fight.

"Acknowledge Concursion," Erin said. "We will get there long before you do, if Daniel's memories in my mind are accurate, so I'll have Kathra roll out the welcome mat and have Ndidi fix something extra special for dinner."

"How's Daniel?" A'Alhakoth asked.

She wasn't sure how she felt about the man. The rest of

the Mbaysey had a low opinion of males in general, but accepted and even liked Daniel. She wasn't sure how she felt about a man who could do those things.

But the tribe was apparently still alive because of him.

Again.

"Unconscious but stable," Erin said, almost evasively. "We'll know better in three days."

Three days?

Even a SkyCamel could have made it to Concursion in that time. What had happened to the man when the Sept killed his ship? Or were the rumors true and Daniel's life was umbilically linked to the ship? Had the death of one killed the other?

"Understood, Spectre Two," A'Alhakoth said. "We will see you in a few days."

The ship-art-piece was painfully bright to look at out the window. On the sensor screen, it was just a pulsing dot in ways she didn't think screens were supposed to display. It was almost like the sensors couldn't get a lock on it.

But that wasn't possible.

Was it?

And then it was gone.

A'Alhakoth blinked rapidly and saw an afterimage of light streak across her vision, where the lightship had moved. She had never heard of a ship making a jump like that.

What kind of ship had Daniel's predecessor stolen?

"Course plotted," Kamsichor announced in a quiet voice that held as much pride as her eyes did. "Destination: Concursion."

"Take us home," A'Alhakoth replied with an equally proud smile.

FIFTY-FOUR

"Is he dead?" Kathra asked, as she watched a medical team load Daniel onto a cart and start to transport him to the new medbay her brand new ship came with.

That had been one the few places she had upgraded her ship from the raw hull and basic equipment that Trade Factor Isaev had built her.

"I don't think so," Erin replied, falling into step with her as the followed her chef out of the flight deck. "But he also hasn't woken up."

The other three followed, waving and exchanging hugs with the rest of the comitatus, who had been waiting on pins and needles for them.

Kathra glanced back at the *thing* that had brought them to Concursion. She recognized it from the Turtle, but hadn't been aware that it was still flight-capable.

"You don't think so?" Kathra's feet slammed to a halt and she turned to confront Erin.

"It's complicated," Erin said, taking her hand and dragging her to where Daniel was still out cold on the cart.

Kathra didn't resist much as Erin placed her hand on Daniel's, halting the entire procession in the hallway.

"Daniel, it's Erin," she said quietly, leaning down to speak directly into his ear. "Kathra's here."

She wasn't sure what to expect, but suddenly she was falling into Daniel's mind.

There was a room. It suggested a small living room on the surface of a planet, located rather out on the edge of town, with a small, fenced in yard visible through a picture window.

Daniel was seated on a cloth-covered couch, looking like he had just woken up from a six-day bender and dressed in simple black cotton.

"What happened?" she asked.

Rather than speak, memories flooded her mind. Urid-Varg attacking the ishtan and destroying most of them. the, stalking the conqueror, and then stalking Daniel. Capturing him and the four women and carrying them to the Turtle so the ishtan could destroy it as well.

The air around her turned cold and dark, like stories always suggested, just before lightning struck. Yet another reason she didn't live on a planet.

Daniel seemed reticent to continue, so Kathra pushed. He could be like that. Stubborn, but only when he thought he was protecting someone else from pain or indignity.

She was still at least as tough as he was, but new facets of the man were seemingly revealed every day.

The pain of the Axial Megacannon slamming into the Turtle was the worst thing she could ever imagine, even worse than that childbirth still sometime in her future. Three times it hit, blasting holes in the previously-impenetrable shell and wreaking havoc inside.

Finally, the Turtle itself died.

Others might question it, but Daniel had been inside the

thing's primitive mind at that very moment when the overload of pain and agony caused it to surrender life itself.

Daniel had only held on by the thinnest of threads. Looking back at him now, seated in the couch while she was in a nearby chair, she wasn't sure he wanted to live.

"I had to get them home," he said quietly, as though even breathing hurt, let alone talking. "I owed them that much."

"Daniel, we owe you more than you will ever understand," Kathra replied. "Your body is on my new warship, custom-built and a vast improvement over *WinterStar*. You have saved us now several times, and revealed many of my enemies who thought to move in secrecy. You are Mbaysey, now and forever. Even if you chose to leave us at some future point, that will not change."

Some of the pain on his face faded.

"I failed," he said, speaking mostly to himself.

"How?" she snapped, anger rising up now, since that seemed to be the thing he needed. "You were overwhelmed by six of them, yes. They knew that they could handle you, or they never would have played such games to draw you in. What they never appreciated was how stubborn Iruoma really is. And she killed two of them, so the four remaining won't be strong enough to take you again, except by surprise. And they can't hold you. My own memories show that."

"The Turtle is gone," he whispered. "All that wealth would have transformed the Mbaysey. All that history gone forever."

"Urid-Varg lived in his own past," Kathra pointed a sharp, accusing finger at him. "Reliving the glories lost, rather than seeking new adventures. Even attacking the Mbaysey was just him trying to find something to excite him, after he had grown inward and strange. You would do the same if you never left your kitchen again."

"I shouldn't," he said, rising somewhat to her anger. "Look at what I've done."

"What have you done, Daniel?" Kathra asked. "I've seen your memories as well as the many creatures you have stolen them from. The Left Hand of Evil? You are nothing like them. I only have to witness the slightest bit of Urid-Varg's life, or the ishtan to know that. You work hard not to let the power you have corrupt you, although I can see that I'm going to have to force you to spend more time in the front of the house, so you can't wait out the rest of your life hiding behind your pots and pans from the rest of us."

"I failed."

"You survived," she said. "You brought Erin, Iruoma, Kam, and Nkechi home. A'Alhakoth, Kamsichor, and Adanne are a day behind you, also safely escaped. The only thing I lost was *WinterStar*, Daniel. The Star Turtle was always a larger problem, threatening to divide the Mbaysey and the comitatus. And I expected it to eventually drive you away, where you would most likely turn into another Urid-Varg, even if you couldn't transfer yourself on. Assuming that it would be possible, requiring great enough ennui on your part."

She leaned back and studied the room around her. Homey. Warm. She suspected it had been his childhood home. The place he retreated to when he was frightened.

Like now.

"I'm not done with you, Daniel Lémieux," she pronounced gravely. "The comitatus is not done with you, especially as you are the first male ever admitted. It is incumbent upon you to teach other males how to serve, as well as non-fighters like Ndidi how to become warriors. You will return with me to the waking world. Am I clear?"

She could see him squint. Pain, disbelief, or refusal was unclear, but Kathra Omezi wasn't having any of it.

"Awaken," she commanded him. "All of life is pain. Losing Yagazie was the hardest thing I have ever faced, but it could not stop me."

"And the next time I fail you?" he asked quietly.

"Then I will have failed you, Daniel, to have put you there without sufficient help," she replied. "That was my failure before, thinking that five members of the comitatus would be enough. Next time, it will be all of them, myself included."

That finally seemed to get through to the man. He flinched, but it was a different kind. Painful awakening, perhaps, that he was part of the comitatus, now and forever.

"It is good," he whispered.

Kathra found herself standing in the hallway again. Daniel's eyes were open. They still contained all the pain in the universe, but he would not die.

Daniel Lémieux had chosen to survive.

FIFTY-FIVE

A'Alhakoth sat uncomfortably on the bench, seated across the table from the Commander in the primary dining hall. All of the comitatus surrounded them, with Erin and Daniel on her side and Ndidi and Areen next to Kathra Omezi.

"Kamsichor and Adanne inform me that they destroyed all the records remaining on *WinterStar* before the three of you abandoned the ship to its fate," Kathra said.

A'Alhakoth couldn't tell if the woman was smiling, but there was no grand frown. Nothing like Iruoma habitually wore.

A'Alhakoth settled for a nod. She hadn't thought to order something like that, but she had never commanded a starship before, let alone one in mortal combat. Some of her poorer relations were still impressed by indoor plumbing and air conditioning.

Kanus was like that, poised on the edge of the future, but still stubbornly hanging on to the primitive past in places.

"And you killed my ship," Kathra Omezi continued in a deep, hard voice.

Again, A'Alhakoth nodded. It had been the only way she could think of to hurt them, once it became clear just how badly hurt the Star Turtle was, and how overpowering a Septagon would be, to say nothing of all those Patrol craft flying around.

"Normally, losing a ship would be cause for severe punishment, A'Alhakoth ver'Shingi," Kathra's face finally cracked enough to smile. "Possibly enough for me to cast you out of the comitatus and even the tribe itself."

A'Alhakoth caught the smiles on the other women's faces now. She relaxed a little.

"However, you also took on a Septagon by yourself, you three women," Kathra said. "And you commanded them to ram that vessel on your own, as a last act of defiance that probably saved your comrades, not knowing how badly damaged the Star Turtle was."

A'Alhakoth shrugged this time. It sounded so much more noble than the profanities that had been going through her mind at the time. Most of them were unfit for any sort of company except the women, and man, she was sitting with today. And they already knew them, so it was unnecessary to repeat them.

"So let me say good job," Kathra smiled now. "I already knew you had what it took to join us. Hopefully, you have finally proven it to yourself as well."

Hands reached out now. Touch. Slaps on the back. Pokes. However these women personally conveyed their own support and welcome.

It still felt strange to belong to a sisterhood of alien women, but that was just because none of them were blue.

She had come home.

FIFTY-SIX

Pasdar had ordered the destruction of *WinterStar*. Not as a navigational hazard, but as a final insult to the women who had thought that they might attack a Septagon, rather than surrendering to it. The Axial Megacannon had liberated all its energy on the ship and shattered it into a small plasma cloud that would eventually fall into the nearby sun.

The infamous Star Turtle that had so haunted Septagon Uwalu was dead. It tumbled through space, already beginning to heat as the atmosphere of the orange star reached out. He would have given much to find a way to salvage the vessel and her secrets, but they had hours, not months. It would be enough to stand off at a safe distance and watch the vessel succumb to the heat.

And perhaps Kathra Omezi might return, hoping for some final heroics. The Axial Megacannon was charged and prepared to shatter her new warship, or any of her friends that wished to die today.

"Aspbad, we are detecting a power signature from the wreckage of the alien vessel," one of the men spoke up suddenly.

Pasdar was out of his chair almost as fast as Rostami, both of them gathering over the shoulders of the man who had spoken.

"Threat?" Rostami asked. From the tone, Pasdar knew he was on the verge of unleashing all the secondary weapons, from the Ram Cannons down to the shortest-range beams, just in case.

"Negative, sir," the man paused to double-check his screens before looking over his shoulder. "If this is correct, it appears to be a class of light cargo shuttle commonly called a SkyCamel, Aspbad. Just emerging from the starboard forward fin."

"Order it to surrender," Pasdar overrode his friend and subordinate. "Destroy them if they hesitate, before they can escape us."

"Yes, Naupati."

"Communications, I have a signal," another voice spoke up. "I think."

Pasdar got there before Rostami did.

"You think?" he demanded. "Let me hear it."

"Stand by, Naupati."

Greetings, Naupati Amirin Pasdar. We are the ishtan.

Pasdar wasn't sure he was hearing this sound with his ears or his bones. It was unlike anything he had ever encountered in a lifetime of service to the Sept.

We share an enemy, Naupati Pasdar, they continued in a weird harmonic that sounded like several voices speaking, rather than just one. *Kathra Omezi and Daniel Lémieux.*

The cook? What kind of creatures were these that they needed to annihilate a cook?

Hunters, Naupati Pasdar, they seemed to reply to his thoughts, as he didn't think he had spoken. *Lémieux is capable of an evil the modern galaxy is unprepared to resist. He must be destroyed. Omezi will shelter him, so we find ourselves with a confluence of interests. We would aid you in hunting down the Mbaysey and seeing both of those humans ended. Are you interested?*

"Scan that vessel," Pasdar ordered.

He looked around, and noted that Rostami seemed to be hearing this as well, whatever it was. Maybe the two of them hadn't just fallen into complete insanity after all.

"Four life forms, Naupati," the sensors desk replied.

Pasdar walked over to look down on the screen displaying the information.

Snakes, but with upper arms, however spindly. Triangular symmetry starting at the snout and running all the way to a fur-covered tail. Enormous creatures, as well, approaching eight meters when pulled straight, if he was reading this correctly.

Ishtan.

Somehow, he knew there would be no record of such a species in any database he wished to consult. He had stepped past that bright edge of civilization that the Sept cast around them like a searchlight. They were into the darkness of the rest of the galaxy now.

And it was up to him to illuminate these shadows.

Can we assist you in your mission, Naupati Pasdar? they asked again.

Destroy Omezi? And whatever her cook had done to warrant such rage as he could taste in the mental images that these creatures imbued into their voices?

"We will talk," he replied.

READ MORE!

Be sure to read all five books in the Star Tribes series.

WinterStar
SeekerStar
SeptStar
SwiftStar
MorningStar

Available from your favorite retailers!

ABOUT THE AUTHOR

Blaze Ward writes science fiction in the Alexandria Station universe (Jessica Keller, The Science Officer, The Story Road, etc.) as well as several other science fiction universes, such as Star Dragon, the Dominion, and more. He also writes odd bits of high fantasy with swords and orcs. In addition, he is the Editor and Publisher of *Boundary Shock Quarterly Magazine*. You can find out more at his website www.blazeward.com, as well as Facebook, Goodreads, and other places.

Blaze's works are available as ebooks, paper, and audio, and can be found at a variety of online vendors. His newsletter comes out regularly, and you can also follow his blog on his website. He really enjoys interacting with fans, and looks forward to any and all questions—even ones about his books!

Never miss a release!
If you'd like to be notified of new releases, sign up for my newsletter.

I will never spam you or use your email for nefarious purposes. You can also unsubscribe at any time.

http://www.blazeward.com/newsletter/

Connect with Blaze!

Web: www.blazeward.com
Boundary Shock Quarterly (BSQ):
https://www.boundaryshockquarterly.com/

ABOUT KNOTTED ROAD PRESS

Knotted Road Press fiction specializes in dynamic writing set in mysterious, exotic locations.

Knotted Road Press non-fiction publishes autobiographies, business books, cookbooks, and how-to books with unique voices.

Knotted Road Press creates DRM-free ebooks as well as high-quality print books for readers around the world.

With authors in a variety of genres including literary, poetry, mystery, fantasy, and science fiction, Knotted Road Press has something for everyone.

Knotted Road Press
www.KnottedRoadPress.com